CAPTIVA HIDEAWAY

CAPTIVA ISLAND
BOOK EIGHT

ANNIE CABOT

CABOT PUBLISHING GROUP

ISBN ebook, 979-8-9894164-0-0

ISBN paperback, 979-8-9894164-1-7

CHAPTER 1

*I*t was a simple plan. Go to Captiva Island and stay at her best friend Chelsea Marsden's home to recover from the loss of her marriage and subsequent death of what would have been her soon-to-be ex-husband.

The turquoise waters, shell-covered beaches, and warm sand was the perfect place for introspection, meditation, and to heal her broken heart. At least that's what Maggie Moretti told herself.

She wasn't Maggie Moretti back then. Back before her world turned upside down she was Maggie Wheeler, loving and devoted wife of over thirty years to Daniel Wheeler.

Once she reached Captiva Island, she felt the weight of the world lift off her shoulders. She was free. Free from what she hadn't a clue, but free to find her way one step at a time, and that was enough.

Her plans evolved as time went on. She never imagined that one day she'd open a bed and breakfast on the island, move away from most of her children and grandchildren, fall in love once again, and claim a new life that she alone controlled.

As silly an idea as staying on the island and resurrecting an inn was, Maggie didn't care what people thought. She'd fallen in love with the property, its previous owner, and eventually, Paolo Moretti, the groundskeeper and owner of a garden nursery on Sanibel Island, in that order.

It was a shocking move to everyone, including Maggie. Didn't she need time to be alone for several years before landing in a marriage so soon after Daniel? Wasn't she crazy to find love in the middle of finding herself?

She'd made some bad choices in her life, and initially, those questions haunted her and made her question her judgment and perspective. But, as time passed, Maggie decided that not accepting Paolo's proposal might be another bad choice, and she didn't want to take the chance of missing out on a beautiful relationship.

The biggest shock to her was that she would trust a man with her heart after everything she'd been through. She made fun of herself back then, repeating a mantra of a man-hating, untrusting and independent woman. One who not only didn't need a man but couldn't see how falling in love with one ever did anyone any good.

Whether the island was responsible, or divine intervention, Maggie fell in love and instinctively knew that Paolo was incapable of hurting her. For a woman who found herself clutching tight to her autonomy, Maggie saw the situation as more of a miracle than anything else.

Even though the trip to Captiva four years earlier was a chance to reclaim her life, the move felt more like running away from home, her children, and anything that reminded her of the life she'd built with her husband of over thirty years. It was a crazy, panicked woman who flew to Captiva Island, Florida, and a confidant and strong woman who emerged from the depths of betrayal, confusion, and indecision.

Regardless of her reasons for traveling to Captiva, Maggie fell in love with the island the minute she stepped onto its shores.

Captiva Island was the place she'd vacationed many times over the years with her family. What might have seemed a simple and innocent trip at the time, changed Maggie's life in ways she never anticipated.

Now, almost four years after that fateful trip, Maggie Wheeler Moretti was the owner of a bed and breakfast called the Key Lime Garden Inn, and more importantly, the place she called home.

Had the inn not held such immense significance for Maggie, her current situation might not be so terrifying. If, all those years ago, she'd visited Captiva, met the previous owner, Rose Johnson Lane, heard enchanting stories about Anne Morrow Lindbergh's time on the island, took a few photos and then went back home to Massachusetts, she wouldn't be sitting in Devon Hutchins' office, squeezing her husband's hand and willing her heart to slow down.

"I'm sorry I've made you wait. Maggie, Paolo. How have you both been? The inn doing well? The weddings were fantastic."

Maggie smiled. "Thank you, Devon. Everything has been great since the hurricane."

Paolo nodded. "Yes, we really don't know how to thank you for all your help. You and the people who work for you made all the difference. The inn has never looked so beautiful."

"That's great. I'm glad I could help. So, what can I do for you?"

Maggie looked at Paolo and suddenly felt foolish for making such a big fuss, but she had no choice.

"We've got a situation. It seems that the husband of the previous owner, Rose Johnson Lane, possibly had a child out of wedlock with a former employee of the inn. This was back in 1960. That child is now a sixty-three year old woman who has resurfaced at the inn and is insinuating that she is its rightful owner."

"We have no way of knowing if the woman is really Robert Lane's daughter. He's been dead for about nine years now. Mrs.

Lane never mentioned anything about her husband having another child. She and Robert had one son and he's been gone about six years. We thought you might know an attorney who could best help us" Paolo added.

Devon put his hand up in the air. "Hold on. Before you go hiring an attorney, I need to ask what you mean by this woman... what is her name?"

"Millicent Brenner. She goes by Millie," Maggie answered.

"What do you mean by insinuating? Has Millie made any legal claims? Has she hired an attorney?"

"No, at least not that we're aware of. She hasn't said anything to us other than the day she made a snide comment about how she has more right to live at the inn than we do. Something to that effect, but no, we haven't heard anything more. We just thought it would be a good idea to be prepared," Paolo answered.

Devon put his pen down on top of his legal pad and leaned back in his chair.

"First, I don't think either of you have anything to worry about. If Mrs. Lane was the sole owner of the inn she had every right to sell it to whomever she wanted. It wasn't Robert Lane's property at the time of Rose's death, was it?"

Maggie shook her head. "No. The deed was in Rose's name and she sold it to Paolo before she died."

"Well, if Robert Lane was dead, and the ownership went directly to his wife, I believe that's the end of it. Even if this Millie Brenner is indeed Robert's child, I don't think she has a legal leg to stand on. But I do understand what you're saying. Let me look at my contacts. I have an attorney who might be able to help you. Even if it's nothing more than putting your mind at ease, it would be worth it to meet the guy."

Devon searched his cellphone, while Paolo massaged Maggie's shoulder.

"Everything will work out, honey. Don't worry," Paolo said.

"Paolo is right, Maggie. Don't lose sleep over this. I mean it. Here it is, I'll send it to your phone."

Maggie looked at her phone for the contact information. "Jeff Norvick?" she asked.

"Yes, Jeff's an estate attorney with a focus on real estate. He's your man. If anyone knows the ins and outs of real estate and inheritance law in Florida, it's Jeff."

Maggie felt an immediate relief, so much so that her body wanted to release the tears that were building, but she took a deep breath instead.

"Thank you so much, Devon. I feel awful always coming to you whenever we're in trouble," Maggie said.

Devon laughed. "Don't be silly. We're family after all. You get in touch with me whenever you need to."

He got up from behind his desk, and Maggie and Paolo then followed him to the door.

"We certainly had a good time at my place in Palm Beach, didn't we?"

Maggie smiled and then lied through her teeth.

"We sure did. Thank you again for letting us stay with you during the hurricane."

Staying with Devon and Eliza Hutchins was not Maggie's first choice, but since her daughter Sarah and son-in-law, Trevor, were there Maggie did her best to ignore the inconvenience.

"Let's get together again, soon," Devon said, shaking Paolo's hand.

As soon as Maggie and Paolo reached the elevators, Maggie turned to Paolo and wrapped her arms around his neck, burying her face in his shoulder.

"Please, God, let Devon be right. I can't lose the inn, I just can't."

CHAPTER 2

*A*fter her early morning walk on the beach the next day, Maggie did what she always did…bake. She'd created a comfortable daily routine that even rain couldn't disturb. When she returned from her walk, she hung her rain jacket up in the mud room and toweled the wet out of her hair.

"Why didn't you take an umbrella?" Paolo asked.

"I love the feel of the warm water on my face. I swear I feel more alive when it rains than any other time. You don't like the rain, do you?" Maggie asked as she pulled a container of flour from the cabinet.

"What are you talking about? I'm a gardener for heaven's sake. Water is my friend, well, that and sunshine. If you really love the warm water on your body you should have left the rain jacket at home," he said, teasing.

"I might be silly but I'm not crazy. Did you see how hard that rain is coming down?" she asked.

Paolo laughed and poured another cup of coffee.

Her best friend, Chelsea, arrived just as Maggie turned on the stove.

"Oh, I see I'm early," Chelsea said, shaking the rain off her jacket outside on the porch. "It's raining cats and dogs out there."

"And a good morning to you too. This is early, even for you. What's got you up at this hour?" Maggie asked.

Chelsea dropped her jacket on a chair outside and came into the kitchen. She shook her head and went directly to the coffee pot. "Nope, not telling you until I've had at least half a cup of coffee. If I don't, I think my head will explode."

Maggie laughed at Chelsea's usual drama-filled morning rants. "That bad, huh?"

"You have no idea," Chelsea answered.

"Well, that's my cue to get over to Sanibellia. I've got so much paperwork piled on my desk, if I don't tackle it today, the pile will be that much taller tomorrow," Paolo said.

He kissed Maggie and smiled at Chelsea. "Ciao, Bella."

As he walked out the back door, Chelsea sat at the kitchen table.

"That man is the brightest light first thing in the morning. You're a lucky woman, Maggie Moretti."

"Don't I know it," Maggie said as she placed a large baking sheet filled with scones inside the oven.

Maggie filled her coffee mug and joined Chelsea at the table.

Frowning, Maggie said, "How about you go first, and then I'll tell you my troubles."

Chelsea sighed. "Maybe you should go first."

Maggie shook her head. "No. I can't. What I have to say scares me. Let's focus on your issues first. Maybe as you talk, I'll get up more courage."

"My sisters are coming to Captiva," Chelsea said, her voice reflecting a real concern.

"And this is a bad thing?" Maggie asked.

Chelsea shrugged. "I'm not sure what it is. Historically, my sisters and I have had a love-hate relationship that never seems to change. We're all so different in the most annoying ways."

"Which sisters are coming to the island?" Maggie asked.

"All three. Two things might happen when they're here. Either you'll never see me, because I've killed them and have been put in jail, or I'll be on your doorstep every minute of every day to get away from them."

Maggie laughed. "There's no third option? How about the four of you all get along and are happy to see each other after so many years? That's a possibility, isn't it?"

"Not likely, but I love your optimism. Let's move on, there will be plenty of time to talk about my siblings. What's going on with you that you need courage to talk about?"

"It's about Millie and her trying to take the inn from me."

Chelsea's panicked face reflected Maggie's fear. "She's suing for ownership?"

"No. Nothing like that. It's just, every day when I wake up, I ask myself, is this the day I'm served with papers? Is this the day my whole world falls apart?"

Chelsea reached for Maggie's hand. "Oh, honey. I'm so sorry you have to go through this. I thought you and Paolo were going to see Devon about it."

Maggie nodded. "We did. He doesn't think we have anything to worry about because the property was solely in Rose's name when she sold it to Paolo. Since Devon's not a lawyer, he gave us the name of an attorney to see on the matter, but I'm still worried."

"What in heaven's name for? I agree with Devon. Whether Millie was Robert's daughter or not, it doesn't matter one bit, at least not where legal ownership of the inn is concerned."

Maggie got up from her chair and paced the kitchen floor, checking and rechecking the oven. Wringing her hands, she then went back to her chair.

"Maggie, is there something you're not telling me?" Chelsea asked.

Not sure she should voice her concerns, Maggie hesitated

before sharing her thoughts. She inched the door to the dining room open just a crack to see if any of her guests could overhear her. Comforted that no one was around, she leaned in close to Chelsea and whispered.

"Millie was born in 1960. Back then, DNA evidence wasn't what it is today."

"So?"

"So, it is very possible to prove that Millie is Robert's child, and as such, she could contest Rose's will. It's possible that she might say that Rose wasn't well or in her right mind when she sold the property to Paolo. She was old and very sick, don't forget."

"Oh, I think that's a stretch. Millie has no idea what Rose's health was like. You and I know, but she doesn't. Rose was lucid and sharper than most at her age. I don't think that's even an issue. More to the point, Robert's been dead for nine years. I doubt Millie is going to dig up her possible dead father's corpse. There is literally no way that DNA can be gathered as evidence without that. Even then, I'm not so sure a long-dead body is the best place to get the DNA."

Maggie pulled the scones from the oven and then placed another sheet of the doughy goodness inside. She then went to the back door and watched the palm fronds of the nearby trees fight against the wind and rain.

Without looking at Chelsea, Maggie answered her friend, "There is another way."

"What?"

Maggie turned to face Chelsea. "Do you remember the box of Rose and Robert's belongings?"

"The one we put in the attic?"

Maggie nodded. "There were several items of Robert's, including his hair brush. They can get the DNA from strands of his hair."

"That's if there are any strands in the brush. Have you checked it yet?"

Maggie shook her head. "No. I'm afraid to go up there."

"So, don't," Chelsea said, her voice firm and insistent. "No one needs to know about that box. You and I are the only ones who know what's in it. I'm not going to tell and neither are you."

Maggie's panicked face searched Chelsea's. "I can't do that. It wouldn't be right. Regardless of the inn's ownership situation, Millie has a right to know if Robert Lane is her father. I can't ignore that."

Chelsea got up from her chair and walked to Maggie. "Listen to me, Maggie Moretti. You've fought to create this world that you live in. After years of living your life through your children and husband, you made something that is your own. If that isn't worth fighting for, then I don't know what is. You are going to leave that box where it is, and if you don't, I swear we're going to have a bonfire on the beach that will solve the problem once and for all."

Maggie's body fell against Chelsea's in a defeated motion. She'd fought everything, including cancer, and now she wasn't sure she had the strength to keep on fighting.

"I don't think I can do this anymore, Chelsea. I'm tired."

Chelsea nodded, and then pushed Maggie away from her. Staring into her eyes, she answered her friend.

"Then, I'll carry you until you get the strength you need. I'll help you fight this and whatever else you don't think you can handle. You're not alone, Maggie. You've got me and Paolo and the rest of your family. I've yet to see anything that can beat that."

CHAPTER 3

*T*he next day the sun was out and there wasn't a cloud in the sky. Paolo and a young man who had just started working at Sanibellia walked around the yard picking up debris from the battering of palm trees from the rain.

She thought about Rose Johnson Lane and wondered what her life was like living on Captiva. Even though Rose grew up in Connecticut, her family spent many years going back and forth to Captiva.

Although Paolo installed their porch swing after they bought the place, Maggie had found pictures of Rose sitting on a swing just like this one back in the day. There were pictures of Rose and other women sitting in wicker chairs sipping what looked like iced tea or lemonade, she couldn't be sure. Maggie imagined them talking about what were the current affairs of the day peppered with a gossip story or two.

A couple of photos were of Rose and her son playing out on the grass in the backyard. Rose bushes were everywhere in the photos and there was even one with her holding up a large pair of hedge shears in front of the house.

Rose loved her flower garden, and Paolo worked very hard to

preserve its beauty. Although Maggie loved to garden, she often admitted that the Key Lime Garden Inn garden would never thrive without the loving care of her husband.

Maggie closed her eyes and listened to the windchimes swaying in the breeze. A car coming up the driveway interrupted her quiet. Chelsea almost always walked to the inn, so Maggie was surprised when her friend got out of her car and walked up the stairs to the porch carrying something in her arms.

"Here, I got this for you," Chelsea said as she threw a yoga mat at Maggie's feet.

"What is this?" Maggie asked.

"It's a yoga mat."

Rolling her eyes, Maggie continued to rock the porch swing back and forth. "I know it's a yoga mat, what I don't know is why you got me one."

Chelsea joined Maggie on the swing. "I bought you one because you don't get any exercise at all. I'm serious, Maggie. You've got to get moving or parts of your body are going to atrophy."

Trying to ignore the insult, Maggie played with the beads on her bracelet.

"I walk on the beach most mornings before you even get out of bed. I'm hardly sedentary. I remember you used to play pickle-ball but then you stopped. After that, I never heard another word about exercise. Now all of a sudden, you're working out and trying to get me to sweat."

"So, I had a brief moment of laziness," Chelsea responded.

"A brief moment? I'd say you had a couple of years of laziness. As a matter of fact, I remember before the cancer diagnosis, I distinctly remember trying to get you to walk on the beach more often. You said the only exercise you wanted to do was carrying your chair to the beach. I said you needed more resistance exercises and you said that every time you get out of bed in the morning, you considered that weightlifting."

"Don't change the subject. And you *stroll* on the beach, it's not the same as a good cardio walk. I don't think I've ever seen you sweat."

"Sweating is overrated," Maggie answered. "Besides, I don't think yoga is the exercise that gets people sweating."

"You're right. That's why I do Zumba, and why I signed you up for a class," Chelsea said.

"You what? You should have asked me," Maggie insisted.

"If I had asked you, you would have said no."

"Correct, and we wouldn't be having this ridiculous conversation."

Maggie could tell that Chelsea wasn't backing down.

"I've been enjoying the class online. Your mother is doing it too."

"My mother is doing Zumba?"

"Yup. She's pretty good too. She says it's because of all the dancing she does when she goes out with her friends. I didn't realize that your mother was so much fun."

Maggie sighed. "My mother is off her rocker."

"Maggie Moretti!" Chelsea yelled. "Show some respect. If you want my opinion, you could learn a thing or two from your mother."

"I have plenty of stuff I'm dealing with right now, Chelsea. I'll get around to exercising one of these days."

Chelsea wasn't letting the subject go.

"You'll see, once you start moving, exercise becomes an addiction. I can't get through a day without it. Maybe we should start you off with the yoga class. Truthfully, I don't think you could keep up with your mother anyway. Not only that but yoga is relaxing. It's like meditation. Zumba is a blast, but it might be too much for you right now."

Maggie wasn't sure if it was the challenge of competing against her mother, or Chelsea's stubborn determination to get her moving, but she suddenly changed her mind.

Smiling, she remembered the times that she and her late husband Daniel went dancing. Those were happier times in their marriage. She was grateful that Paolo loved to dance as well. Until her breast cancer surgery, they'd gone dancing both on and off-island several times.

"Fine. I'll do both," Maggie said.

"You will? You mean you'll do Zumba too?"

"Sure. I assume it's all on video?"

"This class is, but Joni Freeman has a class in person if you want to do that one. I think Isabelle Barlowe is taking that class. It's over at the Southern Seas Resort."

"There is no way I'm taking a Zumba class with Isabelle. We'd get in there and the next thing you know, she'd be kidnapping us on another wild adventure. I'll do the in-person yoga class, but the online Zumba sounds better for me, even if my mother is participating."

Chelsea laughed as she picked up Maggie's yoga mat. "We'll see. Let's go upstairs to your place. We need to pick a good spot for this thing."

Maggie followed her friend across the driveway and toward the carriage house. She had no idea what exercising had to do with relaxation, but if Chelsea was right, Maggie couldn't wait to get started. Anything that would help her handle the stress of dealing with Millie Brenner couldn't be all that bad.

CHAPTER 4

*B*eth Walker rolled over onto her stomach and felt the warm sun hit her back. She raised her body to rest on her elbows and admired the combination of engagement ring and wedding band on her left hand.

"Have you gotten used to your new last name yet?" Gabriel asked his new wife.

Beth laughed. "Not yet, but I do love the name. Beth Walker is just as pretty as Beth Wheeler."

"A pretty name for a beautiful woman," he said as he leaned in and kissed her lips."

"I can't believe we've only got two more days on Maui. By the way, are you going to still love me after this trip? Because I'm sure I've gained about six pounds eating all this delicious food."

Gabriel moved Beth back and forth to get a better look at her belly.

"Now that you mention it, I'm not so sure."

She laughed and punched his arm. "What kind of husband are you? You're supposed to love me no matter what. After all, I'm not going to be this beautiful forever."

"No? You should have told me that before the wedding. Now, what am I going to do?" he teased.

Beth took another sip of her tropical drink and sat up, facing the ocean.

"I bet I'm the only person in the world who thinks seriously about moving to Maui when they're here on vacation," she said sarcastically.

"You and a million others, for sure. I'd move here in a heart-beat if we didn't have so many friends and family back home depending on us. Once we get to Oahu, you're going to want to move there too."

"You might be right. My boss probably wouldn't be surprised though. He knows that when I set my mind to something, there's no changing it. Now that I think about it, leaving my job to move to a tropical island would be far easier than convincing my family to let me go. Mom would be calling a Code Red and gathering the family on Captiva to plan how to fly here to kidnap me and bring me home."

"Don't forget, she'd probably first make everyone a pot of tea."

Beth laughed at Gabriel's words. "It's perfect that I married you because you know how my family operates. You're going to fit right in, although I should warn you that now that you're in the family, it will be hard to keep secrets from any one of my siblings, my mother, or Grandma Sarah. Your life is no longer your own."

Beth smiled, watching Gabriel's face go from cheerful to worry in a heartbeat. She loved teasing him, but she also had to admit that on this subject, she wasn't kidding.

"It was good to see your father at the wedding. He seems to be doing much better."

"I think you're right. It breaks my heart to hear him say that Mom doesn't recognize him at all. At least the last time we saw her, there were moments of recognition, but that's gone now."

Beth could feel Gabriel's pain and wished there was something she could do to alleviate it. Early-onset Alzheimer's disease was a cruel illness, robbing entire families of time with their loved ones. For Gabriel's father, he lived solely for his wife, spending a large portion of his days at the assisted living facility and watching her engage with other people as if she'd known them for years.

Gabriel felt there was little to be done about his father's situation, but Beth had an idea.

"I know it might take some convincing, but do you think your dad might move to the East Coast, to be closer to us and your brother's family?"

Gabriel shook his head. "I can't see that happening. He's dedicated to being with my mother. If he left now, I think he'd feel that he'd abandoned her in her time of need."

"I understand, but the reality is…"

"I appreciate what you're thinking, but I don't want to put him in a position where he has to entertain any other living situation but the one he has now. I know him. If we bring it up, he'll first push the idea away, but over time, little-by-little the idea will eat away at him and he'll suffer guilt for even considering it. Trust me, I've already thought about this."

"I'm sorry, it's just that I feel so helpless to do anything,"

Gabriel put his hand against Beth's face. "I love your heart and I love that you want to help. I hate to even utter these words, but in time, we can talk to him about it."

"When would that be exactly?"

Beth immediately regretted the question. She'd missed his point entirely, and now, a deep sadness entered their conversation.

"My mother won't live much longer. When she passes, I'll talk to my father. He'll need to be near me and my brother when that happens. After all, we're the only family he has."

Beth nodded and then leaned into Gabriel. They stayed like

that for several minutes before she thought it best to change the mood.

"Hey, I'll race you into the water," she said with a twinkle in her eye.

She had barely sat up before Gabriel was on his feet. He reached for her, helping her up.

"How about we don't race, but instead I hold you in my arms?"

Being Beth, she fell into his embrace for only a brief moment before she pushed him away and ran to the ocean, yelling back at Gabriel.

"Just because I'm a married woman now doesn't mean I've lost my competitive spirit."

She laughed watching Gabriel try to catch up, and when he did, he pulled her into the water and under the oncoming crystal-clear turquoise wave.

CHAPTER 5

*M*illie Brenner watched the children run up and down the sidewalk, racing to be the first to reach a telephone pole. Sitting on the front step of her newly rented house, she finished eating half of her sandwich, leaving the other half for her dinner.

She put what was left in a brown paper bag and opened her wallet. Fanning through her money, she sighed. With forty-three dollars to her name, her stomach turned again, this time from fear.

She'd met with an attorney four days prior and hadn't been able to get his words out of her mind.

"I think you've got a real good case, Ms. Brenner. You give me a call just as soon as you're ready to move forward on this. Don't forget, I don't get paid unless you win."

Millie didn't know what that meant. Would the lawyer really get nothing for all his time working on her case if she didn't win? That didn't make sense to her. It sounded more like the kind of promise made by attorneys who often advertised their services on billboards and only took accident cases.

Millie didn't have a clue what she was doing. All she knew

was that she had no money to pursue a lawsuit against anyone, let alone someone so well known and loved as the owners of the Key Lime Garden Inn. Besides, she'd only met with the man because she was upset with Maggie Moretti.

Maggie wanted Millie gone from the inn and Millie was more than happy to oblige. At first, she was hurt and upset, but as the days passed, she decided that she'd find another bookkeeping job and it would be even better than the one at the inn.

Millie chuckled at her foolish thinking because the truth was that she needed more than a job. She needed a place to belong, surrounded by people who cared about her and needed her. It wasn't enough to bring home a paycheck. Without family or friends, she'd sit in her rented house and be just as miserable as she was now, the only difference was that she'd stop worrying about where her next meal would come from.

Before she put her wallet back inside her handbag, she looked at the lawyer's business card. Sean Doyle was a small, frail-looking man, with large, thick-framed glasses that he continually pushed up on his nose as she sat across from him. He stuttered every so often, and his pants looked two sizes too big for his body.

The meeting went well enough, and because she had nowhere to go and no one to talk to, Millie stayed in his office for an additional hour asking questions she already knew the answers to.

Millie put Attorney Doyle's business card back inside her wallet, threw the wallet inside her handbag, scooped up her lunch bag, and got up from the steps. Brushing the dirt off her skirt, she ignored the children who were trying their best to bother her.

"Hey, lady, do you live here?" a little boy with a plaid shirt asked.

Millie didn't answer. Instead, she hurried inside, trying not to cry. She shut the door behind her and locked it, making sure no one could bother her. She threw her handbag onto the living room sofa and then walked to the sliding glass doors and out onto the porch. Looking out beyond her backyard to the right, she watched her neighbor plant flowers in clay pots. It was a warm afternoon and most people in her neighborhood were outside in their yards.

To the left, she could hear a couple arguing. The yelling was a regular occurrence but it didn't bother Millie at all because, although she had never once spoken with them, she was glad to have people near with whom she could reach out if ever she needed help. The four of them, the gardener, the married couple and Millie...her imagined family.

Although few, there were moments from her childhood that she remembered fondly. Her two step-sisters spent some time with her after her step-father married her mother. Brenda and Bonnie were a little older than Millie, but the difference in age wasn't enough to be a problem. When they visited their father, Millie got to have sisters to play with.

When her parents divorced, her sisters stopped coming around. It was abrupt and made Millie feel the loss of family much more than her mother suffered the loss of her husband. Kathleen O'Hara began dating right away and Millie was once again tossed to the side.

Later, in her loneliness, Millie had moments when she considered getting in touch with her step-sisters, but too many years had passed and it felt strange to even think of them as her step-sisters at all.

Millie often pretended that she had more relatives. Even when she applied for the job at the Key Lime Garden Inn, she lied to Maggie about having a family. She couldn't bring herself to either recognize or admit how alone she was.

She kept her personal life as private as possible but understood that people like Maggie Moretti and her family would naturally inquire about Millie's life. That was what was so appealing to her about Captiva Island. She loved the small-town way of life, and it was an added bonus to have such beautiful and tropical surroundings. It was a shame that she couldn't be part of that world.

Unless...

Feeling sad, she walked to the sofa and picked up her handbag. She pulled out the lawyer's business card once again and sighed. There was no point in waiting. She needed to change her life, and fighting for the Key Lime Garden Inn was the only thing she had left to help her do that very thing.

CHAPTER 6

*J*eff Norvick was unconventional to say the least. Everything in his office seemed out of place, and he didn't look anything like Maggie had imagined. A surfboard on the wall behind him, coupled with his long gray hair and Hawaiian shirt had Maggie questioning if Devon might be playing a practical joke on her and Paolo.

"Devon is a great guy, isn't he?" Jeff asked. "We go back a long way."

"Yes, he certainly is," Maggie answered, wondering how well the two men knew each other.

"I do a lot of work for his company, but when we were younger...well, I don't mind telling you that the two of us used to get into a lot of trouble."

Maggie smiled but didn't know or want to know what he was talking about. What she needed were answers to her problem.

"I don't know how much Devon told you, but our situation is keeping us up at night. We can't let this worry continue, so we need to protect our interests."

He smiled. "Your interests being the Key Lime Garden Inn?"

Nodding, Maggie answered, "Yes."

Not to be ignored, Paolo added his opinion.

"The truth is that we're not certain we have a problem at all. Millie hasn't approached us or threatened us except to imply that she has rights to the inn."

Jeff nodded as he took notes. "Devon mentioned that. Something about a long-dead father. What is her name again?"

"Possible father...we don't really know what the facts are around that. Her name is Millicent Brenner," Maggie answered.

Jeff Norvick swiveled from side to side in his chair and smiled. "Well, the truth of it is that it doesn't much matter whether he is...rather, was the father. If I understand correctly, ownership wasn't his at the time you purchased the inn."

"That's right. His wife Rose sold it to my husband initially, then the two of us became the inn's rightful owners."

"Have either of you talked to Millicent about her intentions?"

Maggie and Paolo shook their heads.

"No. I was afraid to ask her. The last thing I needed was to put ideas in her head," Maggie answered.

"Is there any other history of conflict between the two of you and her?"

"Not at all," Paolo responded. "We welcomed Millie into our business to be our bookkeeper and a member of the inn's family. That's how we treat all our employees...as family."

"Paolo's right. We pride ourselves on being close with everyone who works at the inn. I think it's the right way to run our place. We've been there for everyone. No matter what they go through in their personal lives, we're there to support them," she said.

Jeff seemed pleased with Maggie's answer.

"Then I'd like to suggest something. At this point, since there hasn't been any legal filing that you're aware of, perhaps you go and talk to Millie about her situation. See what it is that she's after. It's possible she has no intention of starting a legal battle with you. Maybe there is something else she wants. I think until you find that out, you're going to continue to lose sleep wondering when she'll make her next move."

Confused, Maggie needed clarification. "I don't understand. What else could Millie want from us?"

Jeff smiled. "I've been in this business for over thirty years. You'd be surprised how much litigation could have been avoided if people had just communicated their feelings in a non-hostile environment. The minute you get into the courtroom, the gloves are off and the fight commences, and the judge has all the control. I will tell you, however, that from a legal standpoint, I don't believe that you have anything to worry about."

A tinge of anxiety formed in Maggie's stomach. She wasn't the type of person to back down from a threat of any kind, but she couldn't imagine what she would say to Millie.

"I have no idea how I would approach her. Do I come right out and ask her if she's going to try to take the inn from me?"

Jeff shrugged. "I don't think you need to go there right off. I think it makes sense to let her talk first. I'm sure you can judge where her head is at. By all means, I'm happy to represent you if you need an attorney, and not just because you're Devon's family. I'm interested in this woman and her thinking, and I'd like to see the Key Lime Garden Inn stay in your family for many years to come."

Maggie took a deep breath and tried to calm her nerves. "Thank you. That makes me feel a bit better."

Paolo took Maggie's hand and looked at the attorney. "Whatever comes, Maggie won't have to fight this battle alone. We've got one large, supportive family, and an abundance of friends on the island. We'll get through this together, like we always do."

They thanked Jeff and as they made their way to the door, Jeff shook Paolo's hand, and looked at Maggie.

"You know, as soon as you walked into my office, I could tell that you were a strong woman. I'm glad to see that my initial instincts were right. Stay positive."

Maggie smiled. "Thank you. Let's just hope that Millie Brenner feels the same way."

They walked out of the attorney's office holding hands but said nothing. It was as if she and Paolo were trying to absorb what Jeff Norvick said. When they got to the car, Maggie leaned against it, and looked at Paolo.

"What do you think about what he said? Do you really think it's a good idea after I fired Millie, to now go face-to-face with her once again? Won't it feel like I'm confronting her? Is it an aggressive move?"

Paolo shrugged. "Honestly, honey, I don't know what the right thing to do is, but I agree with Jeff on trying to keep it out of court. I say whatever we have to do to ensure it doesn't become a legal battle, we do...and quickly."

CHAPTER 7

*C*helsea wouldn't take no for an answer. "I'm going with you and that's the end of the discussion."

Paolo jumped between Chelsea and his wife and tried to keep the conversation civil.

"Maggie and I will meet with Millie, Chelsea. You don't have to get involved."

A hurt expression on Chelsea's face said more than words could, but that didn't stop her from trying to explain.

"I'm really hurt that you said that, Paolo. I'm a member of this family too. Well, I might not be a legal member, but I'm an honorary one. Besides, I think it would be better if it was just us women talking. With you there, she might feel uncomfortable about sharing her feelings."

"And why is that? Are you saying that I'm incapable of understanding a woman's point of view?" he asked.

Frustrated, Maggie stopped them from continuing,

"Oh for heaven's sake. Why are the two of you getting so emotional about this? We've got a situation on our hands and I think it's best that you both keep that foremost on your minds."

She turned to Paolo and put her hands on his shoulders. "I think Chelsea is right."

Paolo tried to continue explaining his point of view but Maggie stopped him.

"Honey, Millie has a lot going on, and what we also know is that she's not a happy person. Try and put yourself in her shoes. She only thinks she knows who her real father is because of something her mother told her. She must feel like an orphan now that her mother is gone and her marriage is over. I have no idea if she has any other family, but it doesn't look like she does."

"When I interviewed her, she mentioned more family in Florida, but I can't remember the specifics," Maggie said. "Whatever her situation, I think that Chelsea and I might be able to get her to open up and share what's happening in her life. For no other reason than to do everything we can to keep the inn, I think we need to try this."

Paolo nodded. "Ok, you might be right, but if things get out of hand, you need to include me. Promise?"

"I promise."

"I'll leave you ladies to plot and plan. I'm headed over to Sanibellia for the afternoon. I'll see you at dinner."

Paolo kissed Maggie and as soon as he left the room, Chelsea leaned in and whispered, "So, tell me, what's the plan?"

Maggie shrugged. "I have absolutely no idea, but I can tell you one thing. I'm calling a family Code Red. I know that you, Paolo and I can handle Millie, but I've got to include my kids. They're going to have a fit with me because I haven't said anything about this to them so far."

"Maybe Beth should be the first person you call. With her legal expertise, she might be a good resource," Chelsea suggested.

"Are you kidding me? There is no way that I'm calling my daughter on her honeymoon. It's bad enough that Chris and Becca decided to put off theirs, I'm not going to ruin Beth and

Gabriel's Hawaiian honeymoon for anything in the world. She can find out about all this when she gets home."

"Don't you think we should meet with Millie first? I mean, what if Millie has no plans to go after the inn? It's possible that including your children might make things worse. It's all about what you can handle. Once the kids know, you'll be on the phone with them constantly. Can you juggle all that?" Chelsea asked.

Maggie nodded. "I hear what you're saying. The lawyer had the same idea, but at this point I don't trust any of this. I need to be absolutely certain that there is no way Millie can get the inn. I'm going to need all hands on deck for this one. Let me send out texts to everyone. I'll put out the Code Red alert and then you and I can drive over to Millie's. I'll schedule the video call with my kids for tomorrow. Give me a few minutes and then we can go."

Chelsea rolled her eyes. "No time like the present, I always say. Good luck."

After Maggie finished her texting, she handed Chelsea a piece of paper with Millie's address.

"Put that in the GPS, will you? I have a general idea of where her place is, but I'm not exactly sure of the location."

"I thought she lived on the island, this address is in Fort Myers," Chelsea said.

"No kidding. When she started working for us, she said she lived on the island but didn't have details on the mailing address. Something about there being a communal mailbox. As soon as I realized she wasn't on the up and up, Ciara and I did some digging. Now that I know more about Millie, I have to assume she lied."

"I'd say so. She didn't strike me as having much money though. Captiva is expensive, as you know."

Maggie wondered how much of what Millie told her were lies. Somewhere in the middle of her lies was a bit of truth, but what that was remained to be seen.

"So what happened with the Code Red? How did the kids react?" Chelsea asked.

Maggie laughed. "I think I'm using the Code Red alert system too much, they're starting to take these things in stride. No one seemed panicked at all. At least, not as panicked as I am. Anyway, we're all getting online tomorrow for a Zoom video call."

"Your kids know you better than you think," Chelsea said.

"What you're saying is that they think I overreact?" Maggie asked.

"Well, let's put it this way. It's one thing to call a family meeting, it's a completely different thing when you call your family meetings "Code Red." I mean just by virtue of the name you're overreacting. Seriously, Maggie? When did you invent this thing? For the kids' sake I hope they were adults when you did."

Maggie put her hand up in the air.

"Don't go there, Chelsea Marsden. I'm a good mother and you know it."

Chelsea laughed. "Calm down. I'm just saying you've been known to be a bit dramatic."

Shocked at Chelsea's observation, Maggie poked Chelsea's arm. "Talk about the pot calling the kettle black. No one does drama like you, Chelsea. Not even me."

CHAPTER 8

When they reached Millie's home, they parked in front of the house and Maggie's heart raced.

"I have no idea what is wrong with me, but I'm a nervous wreck," she said.

"Just remind yourself that you've gone through cancer and beat it. Everything after that is a breeze."

Maggie smiled. "I hadn't thought of it that way. Thanks, Chelsea. You're a good friend. I'm glad I brought you with me."

"Don't thank me yet. This thing could blow up in our faces," Chelsea said with more than a touch of doom.

Millie's place didn't look anything like Maggie imagined.

"This house is huge. How can Millie afford this?"

Chelsea shrugged. "Beats me. She obviously has more money than we thought. This woman is more of a mystery as the days go by. Don't give anything away, Maggie. Let her do as much talking as possible. We don't need to give her any ideas."

Maggie looked at Chelsea. "Ideas? Like what?"

"I don't know, just be careful, okay?"

"Fine, but I think you watch too many of those crime shows on tv. Let's get in there before I lose my nerve."

They walked up the few stairs to the front door and knocked. Within seconds, Millie was at the front door and ready to fight.

"I told you kids to leave me…"

Shocked to see Maggie and Chelsea standing in front of her, Millie froze in place.

"Hello, Millie. We thought we'd stop by and see how you're making out," Maggie said.

Millie's eyes moved back and forth between Maggie and Chelsea, and then down at the ground, seemingly uncomfortable with making eye contact.

"I'm fine." She looked up again at Maggie. Her tone defiant, she continued.

"Not exactly Captiva Island, is it?"

Without taking the bait, Chelsea interrupted her, "May we come in, Millie? We'd like to visit with you for a bit if that's okay."

Reluctantly, Millie opened the door and stepped aside, making room for Maggie and Chelsea to enter.

"I don't have anything but water to offer you. Would you like a glass?" she asked.

Maggie shook her head, and Chelsea did the same. "No, thank you," Maggie answered.

"Nothing for me," Chelsea added. "May we sit?"

Millie nodded. "Yes."

All three women took a seat as Maggie looked around the living room and at the open-concept dining and kitchen area. The rooms were uncluttered and seemed minimalistic to her. It was almost as if no one actually lived in the home.

"Do you own this place?" Maggie asked and then, as if she'd done something wrong, received a shake of the head from Chelsea.

Millie didn't hesitate. "This is a temporary situation. I'm renting for the moment."

The implication of her provisional lodgings hung in the air, so Maggie decided to ignore Chelsea's warning, and pushed further.

"Why is this temporary?" Maggie stared into Millie's eyes. "What's next for you, Millie?"

Millie seemed to hesitate, almost searching for courage. She met Maggie's stare with her own.

"Truth is what I'm seeking. Right now, my focus is on finding out more about my father. Everything I know, I got from my mother's stories. I've believed everything she ever told me, but I need legal proof before I do anything else. It matters to me."

"I can understand that. I just don't know how you'll accomplish it. Short of digging up Robert Lane's grave for DNA…"

Millie shook her head. "No, that won't work. He's been gone too long now. That much I know. I need to find something of his or someone who is still alive and related to him." She leaned in toward Maggie. "Are you sure that you can't help me? The Lane family must have left items behind for the sake of history if nothing else."

Maggie didn't dare look at Chelsea for fear that she'd give herself away. Reminding herself that whatever she'd packed away in the attic would stay hidden from everyone, especially Millie Brenner.

"I'm sorry, Millie. We had a dumpster and threw most things away. You've already seen many of the photographs of the family back then. Any other artifacts we chose to keep are on display under glass in the library. You're certainly welcome to look at those things again; otherwise, I'm afraid that's all I can do to help you."

Millie didn't look convinced, and Maggie's stomach suddenly churned with the fear of being found out. Just then, Chelsea stepped in and saved Maggie from losing her poker face.

"Millie, you didn't answer Maggie. Why is staying here only temporary? What are your plans beyond trying to find out if Robert Lane is your father? As a matter of fact, let's say we find that you are indeed Robert Lane's child. What happens after that?"

Maggie's face felt warm.

Millie looked at Chelsea and then back at Maggie. "If I'm Robert Lane's daughter, then I should have been able to inherit his estate. Obviously, my half-brother is dead, so that leaves me. Whatever he owned, should have gone to the next of kin."

"Including, I suppose, the Key Lime Garden Inn?" Chelsea asked.

Millie looked embarrassed but held her chin up and answered.

"Of course. The Key Lime Garden Inn should go to me."

Maggie jumped up from her chair and Chelsea held her back from what looked to be a physical confrontation she hadn't anticipated.

"The Key Lime Garden Inn closed years ago. Rose Johnson Lane sold the property to my husband and me. It was the two of us who rebirthed that inn. Your name is nowhere on the deed or listed as next of kin. You can make all the claims that you want, but the inn is, and always will be, mine."

Millie stood and then walked to the front door. She opened it and looked back at Maggie and Chelsea.

"I guess we'll have to see about that," she said.

Chelsea pulled Maggie out of the room and toward the door. "Come on, Maggie. Let's go home."

Without taking the time to cool off, Maggie made a rash decision. Before they made it to the car, Maggie turned and looked at Chelsea.

"I'm calling the kids right now. I can't wait until tomorrow. This is urgent," she announced.

Chelsea leaned against the car and sighed. "Of course you are. Why not make a terrible situation even worse by making the kids think something terrible has happened?"

"Something terrible is happening!" Maggie yelled, close to tears.

Chelsea grabbed Maggie's arms and tried to steady her friend.

"I hate to remind you that you've gone through cancer and so much worse than what you're dealing with right now. I know it feels like your world is falling down around you, but it's not. Now, take a few deep breaths and get in the car before you have a nervous breakdown in front of Millie's house."

"You're being sarcastic, aren't you? I can always tell when you think I'm losing my mind."

Maggie could tell that Chelsea was frustrated and losing patience with her.

"Get in the car, Maggie," she demanded. "I think I see Millie looking out the window. Get in the car, now."

Maggie did as Chelsea asked but first, she searched for Millie in the window. A slight shadow reflected against the window moved and then Millie's face appeared.

Startled at the intensity of Millie's glare, Maggie felt unnerved but not afraid. There was something different about the woman, something Maggie hadn't recognized weeks ago when she fired her. Not even the Millie's effort at intimidation could convince Maggie otherwise.

Millie's look was neither threatening nor defensive. Instead, Maggie could see sadness on Millie's face. She got into the car and continued to look at the house as they pulled away.

"You'd better tell me what's going on in that head of yours, because something is brewing and I'd like to know if I'm about to be your partner in crime once more."

Maggie shook her head. "No, nothing's brewing. It's just..." Maggie hesitated. She wanted to say exactly what she was thinking, but feared Chelsea would complain that Maggie wasn't taking Millie seriously enough.

"I don't know. It's just that something doesn't feel right."

Chelsea tried to keep her eyes on the road but turned to look at Maggie several times.

"Huh? What are you talking about?" she asked.

"I'm not sure, but I don't think Millie is going to pursue a legal battle against me."

"What? Why do you say that? Did you not just hear her tell you exactly what her plans are?"

"Call it intuition, call me crazy, I don't know, it's just…well, did you see how sad she looked in the window? It was like she was trying her best to appear tough and combative. She seems more like a broken child than anything else."

Chelsea shook her head. "She is obviously not doing well, but that's no reason to let your guard down. Broken or not, Millie is still a threat."

Maggie wasn't so sure. On the ride home she listened to everything Chelsea said but couldn't shake the feeling that something was driving Millie Brenner's behavior, something other than anger. Maggie chalked it up to years of reading between the lines whenever one of her children had something bothering them. They almost never came right out and said what was on their mind.

It became a family joke that Maggie's teapot was at the ready whenever a serious conversation between her and her children was needed. She believed that a cup of tea always warmed the body and relaxed the mind. Maggie felt that her tea was magic and made people slow down, sit for a spell, and confess without hesitation.

As she looked out the window of the car, she wondered if a good hot cup of tea and a long conversation might solve Millie's problems, and her own as well.

She smiled as Chelsea rambled on from subject to subject. First, warning of Millie's supposed manipulation, and then sharing her anxiety about her sisters' pending arrival.

Maggie thought a cup of tea might be in Chelsea's future

when they got back to Captiva. Not that Chelsea ever had trouble sharing what was on her mind, but Maggie needed to calm her best friend down, and find a way to relieve her own tension as well.

A cup of tea and some time on the back porch swing ought to do it.

CHAPTER 9

*W*hen the text from her brother Christopher came through, Beth jumped off the bed.

"What is it?" Gabriel asked.

"My mother is calling a Code Red."

"Code Red?"

Beth turned and hit Gabriel's leg. "You know about our Code Red alert system. I told you about this a while ago. Don't you remember Mom's Code Red when Michael was shot?"

"Oh, right. Does this mean something as big as that has happened?"

Beth threw her cellphone on the bed and looked at her husband. "It looks like someone is trying to sue Mom and Paolo for the inn. Something about an inheritance with the previous owner's child. I think this woman is contesting the will."

Gabriel sat up and moved closer to Beth. "That doesn't sound good at all. When is the video call?"

"In exactly one hour. Nine o'clock our time, three o'clock theirs. Chris just sent me the link."

"You better get in the shower. I'll call room service and get a large pot of coffee. We're going to need it."

"So much for going to Restaurant 604. I was really looking forward to their Bloody Mary. It's even got a piece of steak on the stick."

"Don't worry about it. We've got plenty of time to enjoy Oahu. Maui was beautiful but I'm really looking forward to seeing as much of this island as we can. Promise me that whatever happens on this video call, we're still heading over to the Pearl Harbor tour."

"What are you talking about? Of course we're going."

Gabriel smiled. "I know my wife. If there is legal trouble, you're going to consider cutting the honeymoon short. All I'm saying is that there is plenty of time to get down to Captiva if you need to, but not until after we've had these few days to explore this island."

Beth put her hand on Gabriel's face. "Don't you worry about a thing. We're not leaving this island until I've had that Bloody Mary."

―――――

"What do you mean you told Beth about the call? Your mother specifically said she didn't want to bother Beth on her honeymoon," Becca said.

"No one told me not to text Beth," Christopher insisted.

"Seriously, Chris? You couldn't have figured that out for yourself? Your mother's so not going to be happy about it when Beth's face shows up on the monitor."

"Listen, you're a Wheeler now, when Mom calls a Code Red everyone...and I mean everyone...is supposed to show up. Otherwise it's not a Code Red."

Becca tried to suppress a giggle, but the entire situation seemed absurd to her.

"When my family has a crisis, we just call each other up or meet over a few beers. When your family has a major issue, you all act like you're in the military. It's crazy. I mean, do you have to report in and salute when the meeting starts?" Becca teased.

"Make fun all you want. This is serious. Someone is trying to take the Key Lime Garden Inn away from Mom and Paolo. I think it warrants a bit of panic."

Becca ran to Christopher and wrapped her arms around him.

"I'm sorry. I'm just teasing you. I know this is scary for your mother and I'm glad everyone is going to be on the call. I'm sure after we all hear the details together we'll find a solution. Your mother has worked too hard to make the inn what it is today."

Christopher nodded. "Thanks, honey. It's times like these I wish we all lived closer. Anyway, I'm sure Beth is happy that I let her know."

Becca smiled. "Forgetting about your mother's desire to leave Beth and Gabriel out of it, your sister would kill you, and I mean literally beat you up, if you hadn't let her know."

They both laughed at the truth in Becca's words. Fortunately, he averted the wrath of his big sister by contacting her. Regardless, he didn't look forward to the scolding he was about to get from his mother.

Lauren couldn't wait to get home from work. She left her real estate office earlier than usual so that she could pick up her grandmother. Grandma Sarah was perfectly capable of driving herself to Lauren's place under normal circumstances, but her car was being repaired and a sprained ankle meant she shouldn't drive, regardless of her insistence that she could.

The Code Red video call was an important family event and her grandmother insisted that she be a part of the meetings every time.

Waving from her front steps, Grandma Sarah walked toward Lauren's car, refusing to wait for assistance.

"Grandma, what are you doing? I thought we agreed ever since you sprained your ankle that you'd use the cane."

"Oh, that ugly thing? I don't know why they make those things like that. You'd think the only people who use a cane are old men with one foot in the grave and the other on a banana peel. That's a business I should start."

"What business?"

"Making attractive and feminine canes for women of a certain age."

Lauren wasn't sure what her grandmother meant by a certain age, but she didn't bother to ask for clarification.

"Lean on me and I'll help you into the car," Lauren said.

"You know, if my car wasn't in the shop, I'd be driving to your house myself, ankle sprain or not."

Lauren said nothing and nodded which was her most recent strategy for responding to her grandmother's outrageous and sometimes over-the-top comments.

When they got to the car, her grandmother pushed Lauren away and got herself inside. Once Grandma Sarah was settled, Lauren went to the driver's side and got behind the wheel.

Although wanting to be included, Grandma Sarah was still irritated about having to leave her house.

"So, tell me what this Code Red is all about. It's getting to the point that my daughter is sending out alarm signals all the time these days. What's the emergency?"

"A woman has come forward to claim the Key Lime Garden Inn as her own. She's the previous owner's daughter. That's all I know," Lauren answered.

Grandma Sarah wasn't one to become worried about much these day, but Lauren's information made her twitch.

"What in the world? How is it that your mother didn't know about this woman before she took over the inn?"

Lauren sighed. "That's all I know, Grandma. We'll just have to wait until we talk to Mom."

41

The disturbing news was enough to silence her grandmother for the rest of the drive home. Lauren hated what was happening to her mother and step-father, but she didn't mind that the shock kept Grandma Sarah from babbling on every time she had a thought.

Lauren and Jeff were excited about her pregnancy but her first trimester drained her with daily nausea and fatigue. Whatever was going on in Florida, Lauren would support her mother as best she could from Massachusetts, but these days, with her energy sapped, she was lucky to get out of bed every morning.

CHAPTER 10

Chelsea joined Maggie, Paolo and the rest of her family on the video call. Paolo invited his sister Ciara as well since she had several interactions with Millie when they worked together on the inn's bookkeeping records.

All of Maggie's children were present on the video call. With the exception of Michael's wife, Brea, even their spouses showed up.

"Hey, Mom. Gabriel and I have about twenty minutes before we have to leave for a tour that we booked," Beth said.

"Beth!" Maggie yelled. "What are the two of you doing here? I didn't want you guys to interrupt your honeymoon."

"I'm sorry, Mom, it's my fault. I sent Beth a text about the meeting. I wasn't thinking," Christopher responded.

"It's not a big deal. Let's not waste time. Tell us what's going on," Beth answered.

Maggie explained in detail everything that had happened since hiring Millie. She then explained why she had to fire Millie, and her latest confrontation. Keeping a watch on the clock, Maggie let her children weigh in.

"So, what does everyone think?"

Beth was the first to respond. "Mom, I agree with your attorney. There is very little that Millie can do. I understand her desire to know if Robert Lane is her father, but as far as having any right to the inn, I think she's dreaming."

Lauren spoke next. "Beth's right. The property wasn't even in Robert Lane's name. It wasn't his property at all, so there is nothing for Millie to inherit. Did you explain that to her?"

Maggie shook her head. "No. I didn't get into all that because I was so shocked and angry at her."

"I had to pull your mother out of Millie's house. I thought she was going to slug her," Chelsea added.

"Really, Mom? I would have paid money to see that," Christopher said.

Smiling, Maggie beamed. She had always been the peacekeeper in the family. Suddenly, she felt proud at having impressed her children with her new boxing credentials.

Sarah held little Maggie on her lap and waved to her grandmother. "Hey, Grandma. How are you feeling?"

"Who, me? Never been better," Grandma Sarah responded with a side look at Lauren. It was her way of putting pressure on her granddaughter to not say a word about her sprained ankle, and the use of the ugly cane.

"Mom, Gabriel and I have to go. We're going to Pearl Harbor today and I'm really looking forward to it."

"Of course. Honey, thank you for doing this. I'm sorry if I worried you."

Beth shook her head. "Not at all. I think we all understand the situation better now. Please don't worry. This is not an issue. You and Paolo get in touch with us if there is anything that Gabriel and I can help you with, but I think you're going to be fine."

"Don't let that woman intimidate you. Stay strong and keep practicing your jabs and body shots. Maybe take one of those self-defense classes," Michael said, only half-kidding based on his smile.

"Thanks everyone, but might I remind you that Millie is sixty-three years old. I don't think there is a situation where I'd appear justified in beating up an older woman."

"Thank heaven you said older woman and not old woman. We're not that far behind her you know," Chelsea said, her face serious.

"Mom, why are you at Lauren's? You could have done this on your cellphone. We showed you how, remember?" Maggie asked.

"She's having dinner with us," Lauren answered.

"Oh, that's nice. Does this mean that you plan to stick around Andover for a while?"

Maggie's mother looked like she'd been insulted. "What does that mean? Why should I stay home? You know how much I love to travel. I have plenty of places still to go. I'm just hanging around here until I figure out where I'm going next."

Once again, Lauren kept her mouth shut about her grandmother's need to stay close to home due to her injury and doctor's appointments.

"Well, everyone. Thanks for your support. I feel better just running it by you. Michael, please tell Brea that we missed her. I understand she's gone back to school. How is that going?"

"Well, I think. She loves it even if she is the oldest student in the classroom," Michael answered.

"Seriously, Michael?" Sarah said. "Brea is hardly an old woman. What, is she in her mid-thirties? Oh my goodness, she's ancient. Did you tell her that? I'm sure she'd love to hear that her husband thinks she's too old for college."

Michael glared into the camera at his sister. "I never said she's too old. I'm just saying that everyone else in the class just got out of high school."

"Okay, you two, that's enough. Good to see that you all still have the ability to argue even hundreds of miles away from one another. Everyone go and have a great day. I'll stay in touch."

Laughing, Chelsea added, "Yeah, and I'll call you if your mother gets arrested for socking Millie in the nose."

"You do that, Chelsea. Don't call us right away though. Make her stay in jail for one night at least," Christopher teased.

Maggie turned off the computer and looked at Chelsea. "Tease me all you want but I think that video was a success, don't you?"

"If you feel better talking to your family, then I say it was the right thing to do. The truth is that everyone but Millie realizes that she doesn't really have any legal recourse."

Maggie nodded. "Yes, you're right, but how is she going to get that message? I hope it's not the hard way."

"The hard way? What do you mean?"

"I mean, she doesn't have any money and yet, she's probably going to let some attorney control her next move. Even if she tries to come after me, I already feel terrible for her. She truly doesn't understand what her lawyer might put her through, all in the interest of getting money, probably out of me."

Chelsea shook her head. "Not if there isn't a legitimate case."

"Even legal fees would be unfair, but I still can't shake the feeling that Millie isn't after the inn at all. Everything that woman is doing is for one reason alone, and that's to know who her father is and where she comes from. I've said it before, and I'll keep saying it. Millie is a lost child, and no lawsuit is going to fix what ails her."

CHAPTER 11

The aging driftwood that surrounded the side of Chelsea's house had long ago been carved into several resting spots to watch the glorious sunsets that brought tourists from around the globe to Captiva Island each year. Chelsea never tired of sitting each night on the one piece that her husband Carl had carved for her only eight months before his cancer took most of his energy.

With a glass of wine, she marveled at how each sunset was unique and yet evoked the same feelings and memories. For Chelsea, those memories were of the many nights she and Carl would sit and marvel at the crowds that would come to their little piece of heaven on earth.

The sky often inspired her to paint from the vantage point of her lanai. Hues of coral, purple, pink, and yellow would glide over her canvas in sweeping orchestral motions, and for a brief moment, Chelsea felt as if she and the sunset were one.

The last few weeks were filled with so much activity that she couldn't find time in her schedule to return to her painting. Now, with her sisters' impending arrival, she had little hope of

moments of solitude which, for her, was a necessary environment for inspiration.

"Penny for your thoughts," Maggie whispered.

"Hey, what brings you out after dinner?"

Maggie laughed. "Oh, us old people get out now and then.
Mind if I join you?"

"Not at all. Pull up a stump. Would you like a glass of wine?"
Chelsea asked.

"Yeah, that would be great. You stay put and I'll run inside to
get a glass."

Maggie ran up the stairs and into the kitchen. She returned
with not only a glass, but a bowl of strawberries.

"I found these in the refrigerator. I hope you don't mind, but
it's impossible for me to have white wine without strawberries,
especially when they've been washed and put in this lovely
container. I hope you weren't planning on something special for
them."

"Nope. As a matter of fact, I'm glad you brought them out. I
forgot they were in the fridge."

Chelsea filled Maggie's glass halfway and then added a bit
more to her glass. "So, you didn't answer me. The sun is down
and you scurried inside. What gives?" she asked, teasing.

"I feel bad, that's what," Maggie answered.

"About?"

"About the fact that I'm always dragging you into our family
drama, and I haven't spent any time at all asking you about what's
going on with you. I know your sisters are arriving soon, but I
didn't ask you when."

"Day after tomorrow. That's why I'm sitting here. I'm trying
to enjoy what's left of my alone time. In a couple of days my
house won't be my own. At least one of my sisters, probably Tess,
will be wearing a sweater or skirt of mine, Leah will be eating
everything in my refrigerator and not replacing any of it, and

Gretchen will be on her cellphone fighting with her daughter Kaitlyn about one thing or another."

"Sounds like fun," Maggie joked.

"I'd rather have a root canal," Chelsea lamented.

"How long are they staying?"

"That's a good question. They're headed to Key West. They wanted to stop here first to see me, but then they plan to drive to Key West from here."

"My goodness, that will take…"

"A little less than six hours."

"They should take the ferry from Sanibel. It's quicker. I think it takes less than four hours."

"According to Tess, they want the full experience. They want to drive over the 7-mile bridge and stop in Key Largo. To be honest, I'm surprised the three of them are traveling together. Tess and Leah are the closest, but Gretchen has always gone her own way. I don't see them driving home together. I bet Gretchen will have had enough of Tess and Leah and will fly home instead. I'd bet money on it."

Maggie wiped her mouth with the napkin and took another sip of her wine. Then, she looked up at the stars and surprised Chelsea with her announcement.

"You could always come with me when I go for my scans."

"Scans? What scans?"

"That's how cancer keeps you on your toes. Once you have it, the doctors make you come back for scans every so many months. At least in the beginning."

Chelsea was afraid to ask but couldn't hold back. "Are you feeling all right? And don't you dare lie to me."

Maggie laughed. "I feel fine. This appointment was scheduled months ago. They do this every few months for a while I guess. I keep telling myself that this is just normal procedure, but every time I realize there is potential for bad news. That's the part that really stinks. Even though there was no evidence of disease not that long ago, these little appointments every few months keep you in a cancer patient frame of mind. I hate it."

Chelsea put her arm around Maggie. "You've known that these scans were coming up and you've been dealing with this Millie thing the whole time. No wonder you've been so stressed."

Maggie shrugged. "I'm sorry that I freaked you out a bit when we went to Millie's. I haven't been myself and everything seems magnified a thousand percent." Holding up her wine glass, Maggie smiled. "This helps. Wine, strawberries and my best friend. These are the moments that make all the difference. By the way, Paolo has plans for us tonight so I can't stay."

"You're kidding. The two of you are planning to stay up past eight o'clock? I'm shocked, truly shocked."

Maggie stood and handed her empty wine glass to Chelsea. "Make fun all you want. I'm going home to dance on the beach with my husband."

Chelsea smiled at the thought. "You go, girl. I'm going to stay sitting right here with my memories."

Maggie leaned down and hugged Chelsea. "Carl was a sweet man, and the two of you were really something. I'm glad to see that's still true."

"Go on. Get out of here and have a dance for me."

Maggie skipped down toward the driveway and waved. Without turning, she called out, "Goodnight, Chelsea. Goodnight, Carl."

CHAPTER 12

*B*rea's creative writing class ended just as she remembered Michael's plans to take the kids to visit Lauren and her family for dinner. She'd made a grocery-shopping list in the middle of class but as soon as she realized that she wouldn't be cooking dinner, she relaxed and went to the campus coffee shop for a cappuccino.

It was an indulgence she rarely allowed herself but since going back to college she found that she had more time for herself and small indulgences.

The coffee shop was crowded with students all focused on their computers or cellphones. Most of the tables were taken, so she started for the door, when a man offered her his seat.

"Oh, no, really, thank you but I'm headed home anyway," she said.

"Are you enjoying the creative writing class as much as I am?" he asked.

Confused, Brea wasn't sure who the man was. "You're in Professor McFadden's creative writing class?"

He laughed. "Hard to believe someone my age is a student?"

Brea's face flushed red with embarrassment. "Yes, I mean, no. I'm sorry, I didn't mean to imply…"

He waved his hand in the air. "It's fine. I know you're a lot younger than I am, but I have a feeling that you're not right out of high school either?"

Brea laughed. "You've got that right."

Stretching his hand toward her, he said, "I'm Hudson Porter, student and struggling author, and you are?"

Brea shook his hand. "Brea Wheeler…just struggling I think."

"Well, Brea Wheeler, perhaps we can help each other. Let me know if you need any help with the class. I'm friends with the professor, although that bit of information has little value. The truth is we're neighbors and that gets me zero preferential treatment. However, I do know a bit about what he's looking for from his students. He's a good educator and I think we'll learn a lot in his class."

Brea nodded. "Thanks for the info. I do have to get home though. It was nice talking with you, Mr. Porter."

"Hudson, please. I'll see you in the next class. Have a good day."

Brea walked to her car, enjoying her cappuccino and hoping that Hudson Porter wasn't looking for a best friend in her. She had all she could handle staying afloat with her studies. She had little time for college social life even if it meant avoiding having coffee with a man who appeared old enough to be her father.

The visit from Maggie and Chelsea surprised Millie. She was prepared to take the next step in her legal battle against the Morettis, but she hated that suing them for ownership of the inn was her last chance to better her situation. Maggie's anger frightened Millie.

Although she didn't know Maggie Moretti all that well, Millie never imagined her former employer so upset. Maggie's friend Chelsea seemed equally shocked by Millie's announcement to pursue a legal fight for the inn's ownership but was able to control of her feelings. Millie imagined that Maggie must have brought Chelsea for support but also to intimidate her. After all, having two people confront her was unnerving to say the least.

The first thing Millie's lawyer had asked her was whether or not she wanted to run the Key Lime Garden Inn. It was a natural and logical question and one that Millie never bothered to ask herself. The reason was simple. Running the inn was never her plan. She knew that as soon as the inn was in her possession she would sell it to the highest bidder.

Why anyone would want to deal with tourists and their complaints and demands baffled her. The stories that her mother shared about her time working at the inn did nothing to encourage Millie to run the place. She wanted to know more about her father than her mother's experience as a housekeeper. If that meant working as a bookkeeper at the inn so that she could gather information and do a bit of snooping, then so be it. Running the inn was another matter altogether.

Millie never expected to be fired, although it certainly made sense given the Morettis' concerns. Now, as she exited the elevator to her attorney's office, the butterflies in her stomach made her question if she really understood the battle ahead.

Having been in her attorney's office once before, Millie was unimpressed with its location but had little choice in her selection of a lawyer. The building seemed run down and the neighborhood was equally distressed. She made a note to never be in the area after dark.

Millie walked the hall until she saw her attorney's name, Sean Doyle, Attorney at Law, on the door. As she entered the office, she expected to see him sitting behind a desk just like the first time they met. Instead, he came out from the bathroom wearing an apron and holding a toilet plunger in his hand.

Looking at Millie, he said, "Please take a seat. I'm sorry but I've got a slight emergency in here. I'll only be a minute."

Millie sat on a dark-brown chair that looked like it was made in the 1940s. She remembered how uncomfortable it was the last time she sat in it. It was the only chair in the room and other than the desk, one file cabinet, and a clock on the wall, the office looked empty.

He came out of the bathroom and ran his hand through his hair. Millie found it difficult to focus on anything other than wondering if he had washed his hands.

He sat at his desk and smiled. "It's good to see you again, Ms. Brenner," he said. "I assume you've had time to think about our last conversation?"

She nodded. "Yes. I have. I'd like to proceed but first I need to better understand how your payments work."

"Of course. Well, there is a retainer of one thousand dollars and then as we…"

Millie raised her hand. "Wait. I don't understand. You said that you don't get paid unless we win."

"Well, yes that is true but that is regarding any money you are awarded. If the judgment is ruled in your favor, then my fee will be a percentage of that. However, in good faith, I need to know that you are serious about continuing with your claim. My retainer is typically twenty-five hundred. I think I'm being fair to reduce it in this case."

Millie didn't have one thousand dollars. The only thing of value that she did have was her mother's engagement ring which she wore on her right hand ring finger. She'd have to find a pawn shop and sell it if she had any chance of paying the attorney. The worst part was that it was the only thing of her mother's that she had left.

She looked down at the ring and nodded. "I understand. I'll need a little time to get the money."

"Fine. Fine. Call me when you're ready to proceed and I'll prepare the contract for you to sign."

Millie got up from the uncomfortable chair and he walked her to the door.

"Don't worry, Ms. Brenner. Everything will work out. I'm confident that you will prevail in this matter."

There was little left to say, so Millie nodded and left his office, heading to the nearest pawn shop.

CHAPTER 13

Grandma Sarah turned the tv off and slowly reached for her cane. Her ankle hurt more today than the day before and she wondered if another visit to the doctor was necessary. Frustrated by the slow recovery and potential physical therapy appointments, she threw the remote to the corner of the room and wept.

Crying was not something she did often but her situation was changing and she couldn't ignore her aches and pains any longer. Sarah Garrison had gone through much in her life, and she prided herself on being a strong and independent woman.

Looking around the living room and the stairs leading to the second floor, she finally accepted it was time to downsize. She'd been thinking about it for months but never wanted to mention anything to her family, especially her daughter Maggie.

Grandma Sarah had come to rely on her granddaughter Lauren here and there but she mostly saw calling her as the last resort. It was a slippery slope to a nursing home every time she involved her family. One small discomfort and everyone would start the assisted living conversation.

She rather liked the term "55 plus community." It was accurate, although she knew the truth was that she was closer to 80 minus than 55 plus.

Regardless of her feelings on the subject, she understood all too well how one fall could change her future in the blink of an eye. Continuing to live alone would prove a serious hazard going forward.

Sighing, she reached for her cellphone and dialed Lauren's number.

"Hey, Grandma, how's the ankle?" Lauren asked.

"It hurts."

"Oh, I'm sorry. Do you want me to come over?"

"Yeah, if you're not too busy," she answered.

"I've got a doctor's appointment at two o'clock but other than that, I've got time. I'll be over shortly. Do you need anything?"

"Can you get me a pumpkin spiced coffee? I really like those things."

"Well, it's not the right time of year for those, but I'll see what I can do."

The right time of year. Isn't that just perfect? I'm always having to adjust to the season.

Sarah was tired of the snow and the need to pay someone to shovel her walkway. Sometimes the young man would arrive in time for her to run her errands, but more often than not, she was stuck in her house waiting. She paid him to rake her leaves in the fall, but she had the same trouble with waiting for him to arrive.

The only time her body felt truly comfortable and without pain was when she spent time in Florida with her friends. The warm climate made her feel light and, dare she say it, younger.

There was plenty of money in her investment accounts to buy a property in Florida, and more than once she considered it, but always talked herself out of it for fear that Maggie would control her day-to-day routine if she lived nearby.

Florida is a big state. You don't have to live on Captiva Island.

She hated needing to be looked after. She wanted complete freedom to do what she wanted, when she wanted to, and wondered if it was possible to live life on her terms if she did move to the island.

It wasn't unreasonable to want to be near family wherever she landed, and it was exciting to think that she'd see more of her granddaughter Sarah and her children, Noah, Sophia and little Maggie if Captiva was her home.

Her heart beat faster at the thought, and so, by the time Lauren came through her front door, Grandma Sarah was practically jumping up and down without the cane.

"I was able to get the barista to put pumpkin spice in your coffee. I hope you like it."

Grandma Sarah's face radiated joy and she couldn't wait to share her new idea with her granddaughter.

"By the look on your face, I can tell something's up. You seem in a better mood since our phone call," Lauren noted.

Grandma Sarah didn't bother with the coffee at all. Instead, as soon as Lauren sat next to her on the sofa, she grabbed her hand.

"I need your help. I've decided to downsize and move into something smaller. It's getting harder all the time to manage this house."

Lauren's face lit up and Grandma Sarah knew her news was music to her granddaughter's ears.

"Oh, Grandma, I'm so happy to hear this. I've been thinking for some time now that this place is too big for you."

"Yes. I agree. This sprained ankle has made me rethink things. Do you think it will be possible to get me something with only one floor...maybe a ranch-style home?" she asked.

Lauren patted her grandmother's hand. "I'm sure we can find the perfect solution for you. A house is possible, but maybe something where you don't have to worry about the outside at all. I know some of these places have Homeowners Association fees but that shouldn't be a problem. It certainly is worth it if you don't have to deal with landscaping," Lauren answered.

"You need to help me get rid of all this stuff I've been collecting for so many years. Maybe you and your siblings might want some of it. There are plenty of memories in this house. Can you think of anything else I need to do to prepare?"

"Why don't you let me, Beth and Christopher help you with that? Don't you worry about a thing. We've also got Michael and Gabriel to help move things. With all of us chipping in, I don't think you need to hire help at all. And, let's not forget, I'm a real estate agent. I can help you sell this house and find the perfect place for you. I think Andover has a few communities where you'll be happy. These places have so many activities, your calendar will be filled every week. Have you ever played Bingo? You'll love it."

Grandma Sarah grimaced. "Bingo? Why in the world would I want to play Bingo when I can be hanging out on the beach drinking something with an umbrella in it?"

Lauren's dumbfounded expression signaled to Grandma Sarah that she'd forgotten to explain properly. "Oh, I'm so stupid. I wasn't clear. I'm going to move to Captiva Island. That's where all the action is. I read that the state is ninety-six percent men to one-hundred percent women." Grandma Sarah rubbed her right temple. "Oh, did I say that right? Well, it doesn't matter. The point is that there used to be so many more women than men that it was difficult to find a good match. I think it must be that more women are dying faster than in previous years. In any case, the ratio is pretty good if you ask me."

Lauren's mouth hadn't closed since Grandma Sarah explained her intentions, and her grandmother noticed.

"What's the matter, dear? Are you feeling well? You look pale."

"Grandma, when did you decide all this? You haven't said a word about wanting to move to Florida."

"You're right, but I've changed my mind. When I was feeling

well and able to run around with my friends, go to parties and take vacations, living in Massachusetts didn't bother me because I wasn't around here much. But then, I got to thinking. What happens if I don't feel well or I can't get around as easily as I once did? I'd better plant myself somewhere warm before that day comes. That way, I can still enjoy the scenery and the weather. Good idea, right?"

Lauren nodded. "In principle I would say, yes, it sounds like a good idea."

Grandma Sarah was beginning to get upset. She thought that Lauren would be happy for her, and she worried that her daughter, Maggie was going to have the same reaction.

"You didn't say when you decided to move to Florida, Grandma," Lauren noted.

"I decided after our last phone call. What does that have to do with anything? It's my decision to make."

"Of course it is. I'm just thinking that because you've just decided, you might want to call Mom and talk with her about it. If nothing else, you're going to want her involvement to help get you settled. I can do only so much here in Massachusetts."

"You want your mother to talk me out of it, don't you?"

"No. Not at all. I think calling Sarah and Trevor down there is a good idea as well. Trevor's father owns one of the largest real estate companies in the state. He could help find you something. Please don't get upset, Grandma. Did you take your blood pressure meds this morning?"

"Oh, for heaven's sake. I'm in my right mind, and I'm not sick. I've taken my pills and I'm done with this conversation. I will call your mother when I'm good and ready. In the meantime, you talk to Christopher and Michael and Beth too. Let them know that I want to move before the fall. I'm done dealing with all those darn leaves. Do you realize that the man across the street blows his stupid leaves with that loud blowy thing right across into my driveway and on my sidewalk?"

"No. I didn't know that," Lauren answered.

"Well, I can tell you one thing. If this house sells when the leaves start to fall, I'm going to gather them all up and walk across to his driveway and drop a big bag of them right there. It will be my goodbye gift."

CHAPTER 14

$\mathcal{T}$revor walked into the living room and found his wife Sarah fast asleep on the sofa. Their son Noah and daughter, Sophia, were at their grandparents' house and their youngest was sleeping in her crib. Though he could have managed his paperwork in the office, Trevor decided to come home and do more work at the kitchen table.

"Hey," Sarah whispered. "How long have I been sleeping?"

"Hard to tell. I just got home," he answered.

"What time is it?"

"Six o'clock."

Sarah quickly sat up and looked around the room. "Where are the kids?"

"Maggie is taking a nap and Noah and Sophia are at my parents' place. Did you forget?"

She rubbed her forehead and sighed. "I guess you could say that. Listen, I've got to talk to you about something."

He walked back into the living room and sat on the end of the sofa. "Shoot."

"I need a break."

"Define break."

"Debbie is working out great. I mean she's like a member of our family. I was thrilled when she decided to be our nanny exclusively, and I want her to stay, but…"

"I think I know what you're going to say. You want to stay home with the kids."

Sarah smiled. "How did you know?"

"Oh, I don't know. Maybe it's watching you try to juggle work and family. You're exhausted all the time."

Sarah nodded. "I am, but more than that I feel like I'm missing out on the most important times in their lives. We've got three different ages and at each age they're learning something new. I want to be here for every milestone."

Trevor nodded. "I understand. If you remember, I'm the one who told you to do what's best for you and the kids. I can always cook dinner or do whatever you need to support our family. I want you to be happy. Will you be happy not being at the Outreach Center, or working the Food Pantry, or helping at the Women's Shelter? Only you can answer that."

"Thanks, I knew you'd understand. There's something else."

"Oh?"

"Lauren called me earlier. Grandma Sarah is coming to live on Captiva Island."

Stunned, Trevor asked, "What in the world?"

"I know. Grandma told Lauren and neither Lauren nor Grandma has called Mom yet."

"How do you think your mother is going to take the news?" he asked.

Sarah shrugged. "It's hard to tell. You know how Grandma is. Until Mom moved to Captiva, they lived close to one another their whole lives and they managed just fine. But, I don't know, Mom is different now."

"Different? How?"

"I'm not sure I can explain it but I think in the past Grandma intimidated Mom, somehow. If she tries to do that again, I don't think the result will be the same."

"That's a bad thing?"

Sarah shook her head. "No. Not at all actually. There are moments when Grandma needs to be put in her place. Us kids weren't ever allowed to do it, and Mom wouldn't. But now? Mom is much stronger and not afraid to say what's on her mind. Grandma might think moving down here will be just like it was in Andover, except the weather will be better. If she thinks that, she's in for a rude awakening."

Finding a pawn shop in Fort Myers wasn't a problem. Deciding which one to do business with was the concern. Millie had never pawned anything in her life. She'd been close to it a time or two, but somehow found a way to pay her bills without giving up her mother's ring.

DeWitt Pawn & Jewelry had five-star reviews online, so Millie decided to go there. The small bell above the door rang as she entered and an old man with bifocals greeted her.

"May I help you?"

"Yes. I have a ring that I'd like to get a quote on."

Millie pulled the ring off her finger and handed it to the man. He took it from her and, peering at her over his glasses, he smiled. "The engagement didn't work out, huh?"

"Not mine. It was my mother's," she answered.

"May I ask if your mother knows that you're selling it?"

Millie shook her head and avoided eye contact with the man, trying not to cry. "She's dead."

The man dropped to the stool behind the glass case and shook his head. "You don't want to sell this ring, do you?"

Millie didn't answer. "How much?"

"I can give you eight hundred dollars."

Millie's jaw clenched. "That's all? It's worth so much more than that. Can't you give me a thousand? I need one thousand dollars."

Waiting for his response, she could see him wavering. Mortified but glad for once that someone felt sorry for her, she let her eyes beg for his compassion.

"All right, one thousand dollars," he answered.

She watched him as he went to a metal box and counted out ten, one hundred dollar bills.

Although she felt an obligation to thank him for his kindness, Millie couldn't wait to get out of the store and as far away as she could from her mother's ring.

She left the store and then searched up and down the street, looking for anyone who might see her leave the building. It was a foolish gesture since no one knew her or would probably ever see her again. Still, leaving a pawn shop made her feel like a failure once again. She ran to her car and got inside. Driving to her house she promised herself that as soon as she owned the Key Lime Garden Inn, she'd never see the inside of a pawn shop ever again.

───────

Ciara Moretti swirled the pink colors of her smoothie with her straw as she sat on the steps of Chelsea's house. She called Chelsea the night before and asked if they could meet at ten o'clock the next morning. Her heart beat faster when she saw Chelsea walking toward her. She was nervous and hoped that her friend might alleviate her anxiety.

"Hey, Chelsea, thanks for meeting me," she said.

Chelsea hugged Ciara. "No problem. I decided to take a walk on the beach to chill before I fall apart later today."

"Really? You never strike me as someone who worries about anything," Ciara said.

Chelsea laughed at that. "I guess I'm a good actress then."

"What makes you think you'll fall apart?" Ciara asked.

"My three sisters are arriving this afternoon. The four of us are completely different people and I have no idea how things are going to go with them staying with me," Chelsea answered.

Ciara laughed. "I hear sisters can be a problem. I guess I'm lucky that I only have my brother, Paolo. They say that boys are easier than girls."

"You have no idea, my dear. Anyway, it's good we're meeting this morning. Who knows what things will be like after they arrive. Come on inside."

They went out back to the lanai and Ciara settled in on a plush-cushioned chair.

"Can I get you an iced tea or lemonade?"

"No. Thank you. I'm fine," Ciara answered.

Chelsea didn't bother getting anything for herself, instead she sat across from Ciara.

"Is everything all right between you and Crawford?" she asked.

"That's what I wanted to talk to you about. I'm not very good when it comes to reading the signs that a man can give," Ciara said.

Chelsea smiled. "And you think that I am?"

Ciara's face reddened. "Well, you must be better at it than I am. You seem very wise."

"I'm not so sure about that," Chelsea said, sitting back in her chair.

"I would have talked to Maggie about this, but I didn't want to tell her anything that she might tell my brother. I know she wouldn't if I asked her not to, but I didn't want to put her in that position."

"I understand," Chelsea said. "What exactly are the signs or signals you think Crawford is sending you?"

Ciara hesitated and played with her watch. "I think he's going to break up with me."

Chelsea seemed shocked at her words. "I'm sure you're wrong about that, Ciara. Crawford loves you very much. I think everyone can see it plain as day."

"Then why is he always going off without me and suddenly not around to see me? I'll call him and he asks me if he can call me back in a few minutes, but sometimes it can be hours before I hear from him again. I wouldn't make a fuss about this but the behavior is suddenly different. It's like he's changed somehow. All I can think is that he doesn't know how to tell me and so he's avoiding me. What do you think?"

"I think it's very possible that he's busier than usual. You realize we're in the middle of the busiest season, right?"

"Yes, I know. Do you think I should come right out and ask him if something is wrong between us? Maybe if we talk about it, we can fix it."

Chelsea nodded, "I think that's a very good idea. I also think it's great that you think the two of you can fix it. If there is something wrong, don't assume it's your fault, instead find out what's on his mind, and then talk it out. I think you'll find that you've been worrying for nothing. Do you believe Crawford loves you?"

Ciara smiled. "I do. I really do."

"And you love him?"

"With all my heart," Ciara answered.

Chelsea got up from her chair and walked to Ciara.

"Then, I think this time tomorrow night, you're going to feel much better for having talked to him. Come on, I'll walk you to Powell's. I'm not done releasing all my tension. A good walk around town will do me good," Chelsea said.

Ciara hugged Chelsea. "Thank you so much. I really appreciate it."

The women walked down Andy Rosse Lane together. When

they reached Powell Water Sports, Ciara left Chelsea who continued her walk.

Ciara went inside the store and found Crawford sitting at his desk, his head down looking through paperwork. She took a deep breath and went into his office hoping Chelsea knew what she was talking about.

CHAPTER 15

*C*hristopher rolled his wheelchair into the sensory room and found two children and an adult looking over the newly installed bubble wall. He didn't need the wheelchair much since getting his prosthetic leg, but he felt the kids at Summit Dreams saw him as one of their own when he did.

Most of the children he worked with struggled physically with movement but having gone through the trauma of an explosion followed by the amputation of his leg, he was keenly aware of others who, like him, had difficulty with loud noises, bright lights and sensory overload.

Christopher was able to convince the board members that giving children down time away from the hectic activities in the gym would accelerate their healing. When he presented the idea to construct a sensory room on the west side of the Summit Dreams building, the board members gave him the go-ahead to have it built and have continued their support since it opened.

Now, seeing children decompress in a room that catered to their needs, he felt excited watching them thrive. He had followed his heart and through his efforts, more children's lives improved each day.

He watched as Caleb explored every inch of the room. Kristen, the newest child to come to Summit Dreams for help and rehabilitation, beamed with joy and anticipation.

"Hey guys, I see you've found our newest addition to the place. How do you like it?"

"It's awesome," Kristen answered.

"I love it. I want to be in here all day," Caleb said.

Christopher laughed. "Well, you have to share. Some of the other kids might want to come inside too. We don't want it to get too crowded, right?"

Both children nodded their heads.

"Ok, have fun. I've got to get back to my office and do some work. I'm not lucky like you all who get to play all day long."

The children laughed as Christopher smiled at his assistant before wheeling himself back to his office.

Paperwork was his least favorite responsibility. Interacting with the children was the real reason he'd agreed to run Summit Dreams. Throughout his days at work, it wasn't unusual for his mind to travel back to his past and marvel at how far he'd come.

It didn't seem that long ago when he contemplated ending his life. After his amputation, life had little meaning for him, especially while grieving the loss of his best friend and fellow officer while overseas.

Now, he not only loved his work, but he had also moved beyond the depression and hopelessness, fallen in love, married and found a passion for helping others who struggled with PTSD and physical limitations due to injury or illness. He didn't dare ask for more.

However, the nagging thought that he and Becca should talk about having children of their own felt right. They always said they'd have children one day, and being newlyweds, they weren't ready for that next step, but that didn't mean they shouldn't talk about the future. He needed to think about planning for the right time but had no idea when the right time would be and he didn't want to leave it to chance.

Everything Christopher learned from his experience in the military, and beyond, reminded him that life was precious and fleeting. In an instant, his world turned upside down and he worried that it could happen again to either him or Becca, or anyone he loved.

His focus on the paperwork before him now gone, he decided to leave work a little early and head home. Becca would be getting dinner ready and had an unusual free evening. He figured tonight might be a good time to get the topic started. He didn't need a definitive answer but thought that together they'd be able to come up with a plan for the future.

When he arrived home, the house smelled wonderful and Becca was at the dining room table with a stack of books in front of her.

"Something smells delicious," he said.

"Pot roast. For some reason today, all I could think of was pot roast. I haven't made this in forever. How was your day?"

"Great. As usual, the kids kept me on my toes."

Laughing, Becca asked, "Is that another one of your amputee jokes?"

"I don't know. Is it funny?"

He kissed her lips and then her forehead.

"It's not bad," she answered.

"Looks like you've got a lot of studying tonight. I thought you said you had a night off?"

Becca nodded. "I do. I'm not studying exactly. I'm trying to decide how to schedule my clinical rotations. It's coming up and I need to decide which ones to take first."

"Sounds interesting. Can I help?"

"Not really. I think I've figured it out. One thing that's exciting is that I can officially announce that I've decided to focus on emergency medicine. I love the fast-paced, quick decisions working in the ER."

"That sounds terrifying to me."

"It's where the action is. It feels more my style," she said.

"So that's where you'll do your clinical rotations?"

She shook her head. "Heavens no. That would be a mistake because I need so much more prep before I do that. You only get one shot and I want to be my best when I get to that point. I'll schedule all my other rotations before that one."

"Leaving the most important for the last. I guess that makes sense. I'm glad you know where you're headed. Can we talk about where *we're* headed?" he asked.

He didn't want to sound so serious but since Becca was in planning mode, he wanted equal time to decide their next several years.

"That sounds ominous. I thought getting married pretty much confirmed we're headed in the same direction…no?"

"Of course we are. Everything is fine. I just had some thoughts and wanted to run them by you. How long before dinner is ready?"

"I was just getting ready to put everything out on the table, why?"

"Why don't I pour us some wine, you get the food on the table and we can talk about some of what I've been thinking over your delicious meal?"

"Sounds good," she said, gathering her books and moving them to the coffee table.

She pulled the pot roast from the pan and onto a cutting board. She sliced it and placed the pieces on a platter surrounding it with the carrots, potatoes, onions and gravy. Christopher leaned over her shoulder and breathed in the aroma. "That looks so good."

"Well, if you want any, you'd better sit at the table because that's where it's going."

She put the platter in the center of the table and a large bowl filled with salad sat next to it. Christopher pulled a chair out for her and then went to his chair, ready for dinner and important conversation.

"Ok, so, what's on your mind?" she asked.

"Children." He didn't plan to sound so direct, but it was too late to take it back.

"Children? You mean the kids at your work, or…?"

He put up his hand for no particular reason but somewhere in his gut he worried she'd be on the defense rather than open to the topic.

"Hear me out. We've got lots of time before we're ready to have kids, but we've never really talked about it. I think we didn't discuss it sooner because we were dealing with so much. My leg, your school, Michael getting shot, it seems like our families are constantly facing challenges. As a family we've all been through a lot in the last four years."

"Chris…"

"Let me finish," he begged.

"I know for you right now nothing is more important…well, other than our marriage…than school. I just thought we could talk about when we might add a child to our family. I'm asking you to give me a ballpark…in five years…six?"

"You want me to give you a date when we will have a baby?"

"No….I…well…yes, that's what I want."

He could tell that she tried not to laugh at his awkwardness, but somewhere amongst the convoluted way he approached the subject, he almost laughed as well.

"I know that I sound pathetic. It's just, if you spend time with kids all day, one thing or the other happens. Either you don't want kids at all, or…"

She finally let out a chuckle. "I'm waiting for you to say that your biological clock is ticking."

He laughed and took a bite of his pot roast. "This is going to get cold if we don't start eating."

He chewed in silence and waited for Becca to answer him.

"This pot roast really is incredible. Why don't you make this once a week?"

"Maybe because we're on a budget?"

He nodded. "Oh, right...that."

She reached across the table and pulled his hand away from his plate.

"How about I graduate, and get through at least one year of residency?"

"How many years is that?" he asked, dreading the answer.

"ER residency is maybe three years minimum."

"So, we're talking five years?"

She nodded. "I think we can safely think about adding a little one to our family after that. How does that sound? Can you live with that?" she asked.

He sighed. "I can. Five years is good, not too long, not too short. Plus, we'll have been married for five years and that's a decent amount of time to know whether we like each other or not."

Becca threw her napkin at him. "Very funny."

Christopher winked. "Now, can I eat my pot roast?"

CHAPTER 16

*C*helsea stood outside at the bottom of the stairs and waved at the SUV pulling up in front of her house. Her sister Tess was the first to get out of the car, followed by Leah and Gretchen.

They came to Chelsea with arms extended, screaming their excitement.

"I can't believe we're here," Tess said.

"Oh, it's so good to see you," Leah said, hugging Chelsea.

For some reason, Gretchen kissed Chelsea first on the left cheek and then the right as if she'd been living in Europe these last years instead of New York City.

"How was the drive?" Chelsea asked.

"It was great, except that when you have three middle-aged women in the car, stopping for ladies' room breaks every hour is a thing."

"Yes, and Leah wouldn't always pull into the best rest areas." Looking at Leah, Tess said, "They have those sign things on the road for a reason you know. Anyway, she'd get completely off the highway which added so much more to our driving time."

"It would appear that our sister likes to combine ladies' room stops with visiting tourist locations, especially Civil War battle-fields," Gretchen added.

"You all have to stop complaining. I got you here, didn't I?" Leah said.

"Well, let's get you all settled upstairs. Your rooms are ready for you," Chelsea announced.

Tess and Leah carried their luggage out of the car, but Gretchen was already halfway up the stairs without hers. Chelsea took the subtle hint but decided against taking on the role of her sister's maid and bell boy. Instead, she walked up the stairs and left Gretchen to get her luggage later.

They all made their way inside and went to check out their rooms.

"I remember the pictures you sent of this house. They didn't do it justice. It's really lovely and exactly how I pictured it. You've decorated it perfectly," Tess said.

"Thank you. I'm glad you like it," Chelsea responded.

"Chelsea, this place is gorgeous. No wonder you and Carl picked this spot. It's perfect," Leah added.

"Yes, Carl and I were very happy here, and now, well, this is my home."

"I don't blame you at all for staying in Florida. I've just about had it with the winters up north. I'm glad we're moving to Key West."

Everyone froze except Chelsea, who looked at Gretchen with surprise.

"You and David are moving to Key West?" Chelsea asked.

Just to lighten the mood and slow down the conversation, Leah asked, "Do you have any white wine on ice by any chance? Why don't we all go downstairs and have a little talk?"

Confused, Chelsea nodded. "Yeah, of course. Let's go out and sit on the lanai. There's a beautiful breeze right now and I would love a glass of wine myself."

The women walked outside while Chelsea gathered wine

glasses and two bottles of Pinot Grigio. Chelsea did the honors and when everyone was settled, Gretchen explained.

"David and I divorced four months ago. It's already settled and we've worked out the financial arrangements. Kaitlyn is over eighteen and can live with whomever she chooses. As it happens, she chooses to have her own apartment. She's rooming with two other women...friends from college."

"I'm so sorry, Gretchen. Why didn't you tell me?" Chelsea asked.

Gretchen shrugged. "It's fine. Honestly, it was a long time coming. We fought all the time, so much so that Kaitlyn even suggested we divorce. Can you imagine how bad things have to be that your kid doesn't even want you to stay together?"

Chelsea was inclined to agree with Kaitlyn. As Chelsea remembered it, David and Gretchen weren't a good match from the start.

"So, who is moving to Key West?" Chelsea asked.

In unison, all three women answered, "We are."

Astonished that her sisters were able to ride to Florida together and not kill each other, Chelsea couldn't believe that they now planned to live so close together...maybe even in the same house.

"I don't understand. Tess, you have a coffee shop business and Leah, you've been grooming dogs for as long as I can remember. How can you give up your businesses like that?"

"Technically, we are closing our stores up north, but we're going to buy a property together in Key West and open up a combined coffee shop and grooming spot. We've already looked at a few places online. One of the buildings will house the whole thing. It's together but separate. You should see it, Chelsea. It's adorable."

"Adorable usually means small," Chelsea reminded them. "I'm confused. You're going to have two businesses or one?"

"It's not small at all. It's like a townhouse but we're combining both businesses. We're going to call it Key West CoiffeeShop."

Chelsea spit out her wine and the liquid landed on her coffee table.

"CoiffeeShop? Who came up with that brilliant idea?"

"Actually, I did," Gretchen said, raising her hand. "I thought it was a cute play on words."

Wiping her mouth with a napkin, Chelsea looked at Gretchen. "What is your role in all this? You've been a stay-at-home mom all these years. I don't think you've ever had a job that I can remember."

"Trust me, Chelsea. I did quite well in the divorce. I don't need to work for the rest of my life. I'll be involved but only if I'm bored. I need to relax and enjoy some of the money I got in the divorce."

"So, you're helping to fund this endeavor?" Chelsea asked.

"Well, I can't really help financially, I mean, not a lot of money. I'm giving them five-thousand dollars plus I'll be helping out with working there. I'm definitely a partner."

Chelsea's stomach turned when she realized where the conversation was headed.

"After all, I need to buy a place to live and I don't want some shack of a house. Kaitlyn will need a room when she comes down and knowing her, she won't come alone. I expect kids visiting all the time. Not to mention my friends. That's what happens when you get a beautiful place on the ocean," Gretchen answered.

Chelsea thought her sister crazy for following Tess and Leah to Key West. Gretchen was always the reasonable one but now, she seemed oblivious that her sisters wanted her along for the ride because of the money she could provide. That Gretchen couldn't or wouldn't see that frustrated Chelsea.

"We might as well ask Chelsea what we came here to ask," Gretchen added. "Tess and Leah came to me with this idea and thought that you might want to invest in their business. You probably need time to think, and we're sorry for hitting you with this right away, but it's important that you understand why we stopped to see you on the way to Key West. I mean…oh, that sounds awful. We wanted to see you, of course, but we also thought all four sisters should be in on this great investment. "

Chelsea got up from her chair in record speed; she almost turned her chair over. "I don't need time to think. The answer is no. I live on a fixed income and I can't take that kind of risk."

"Risk?" asked Tess. "What makes you think you'd be taking a risk investing in the CoiffeeShop?"

Memories from their teenage years immediately flooded Chelsea's mind. When their parents divorced, their mother took back her maiden name. Chelsea chose to do the same, growing up Chelsea Lawrence. However, Tess, Leah and Gretchen kept their father's name, which was Kendrick, but the fighting amongst the sisters throughout those years never left Chelsea's heart. It was the reason she chose to keep her distance all these years. She'd found over the years that it was best to remain neutral where her sisters were concerned. It was ridiculous to think they now should join forces on a business deal.

"Not a risk so much as it's underdeveloped at this moment. The three of you can't be certain that everything will go smoothly. It's not like you don't know how to run a business. You've each been successful in your own right. Coming together like this will take time. Right now, I can't invest my money on a possibility. I'm sorry. I don't want this to come between us but friends or family and money don't mix well."

Gretchen looked the most disappointed, likely due to Tess and Leah leaning heavily on her for money.

"What about the bank? Have you all looked into getting them to fund your shop?" Chelsea asked.

"Not yet," Tess said, "but that's probably our next step."

"Actually, there are plenty of financial institutions ready and willing to give you a loan toward this. I think you should check out all possibilities. The Small Business Administration is the first place I'd look," Chelsea advised. "In the meantime, you all must be hungry. Let's get out of here and let me show you around a bit. We can go over to the Bubble Room for dinner. Their menu is extensive and their desserts are to die for."

By all appearances, her sisters weren't angry with her, although she couldn't be completely sure about that. In time, Chelsea figured they'd come up with another plan, and at the very least, would hopefully leave Captiva without tapping any of her friends for money.

CHAPTER 17

*M*aybe it was curiosity, or maybe hedging her bets, but Maggie needed to look inside the box of Rose and Robert Lane's belongings. If she looked carefully at Robert's hairbrush and couldn't see even one strand of hair, she'd sleep better at night.

Chelsea's warning to stay clear of the box was well-intentioned but she wasn't the one pacing the floor at two o'clock in the morning, or feeling nauseous every time she thought about Millie.

Maggie was in the bedroom facing the back of the house. She looked out the window and could see Paolo at the far end of the garden. Satisfied that no one would see her going upstairs, she pulled the attic ladder down and slowly climbed to the top.

When she crawled onto the plywood floor, she reached for the light string. The attic took on a warm glow, revealing several boxes and plastic storage bins filled with family treasures.

She laughed, thinking that her description of these things were treasures. Paolo would disagree and say that most of the items should be donated or thrown away. But like most parents who'd held on to their children's possessions, Maggie found it difficult to part with even one item. Every time she tried, she'd be reminded of Beth scraping her knee when she fell off her bike, or Christopher winning another of his multitude of sport trophies.

Among her memories lay evidence of a life well-lived, bruised egos, bodies and all. There were celebrations as well as defeats and yet she knew that the contents before her were nothing compared to the memories in her mind.

One box however, had more than objects from her family's past. Rose and Robert's box had the power to shape Maggie and Millie's futures, and Maggie's heart raced as she walked toward it. She knelt down and opened the box, pulling out several framed photographs and books. Wrapped in tissue and placed inside a plastic bag were Rose's hairbrush and mirror. Under another tissue was a man's wallet, watch, comb and hairbrush. Paolo had labeled the bag Lane's Bedroom.

Maggie couldn't be sure that one of the hairbrushes was Robert's, but the way it was packaged led her to believe it to be true. She unwrapped Robert's things and examined his hairbrush. There were only two strands of hair on the brush that she could see.

Her heart raced faster knowing that if Chelsea were here, she'd pull those strands from the brush and throw them away. Chelsea's words swam in Maggie's mind, *You are going to leave that box where it is, and if you don't, I swear we're going to have a bonfire on the beach that will solve the problem once and for all.*

Frightened at knowing what she was capable of, Maggie rewrapped the brush and closed the plastic bag. She returned the items to the box and placed the lid on top. Her heart pounding in her chest, Maggie couldn't move. She sat on the floor and breathed deeply, trying to calm her nerves. Whatever the fate of the Key Lime Garden Inn, Maggie couldn't stop thinking about Millie and her desire to know about her father. Maggie had the power to make that happen but to do so meant she'd run the risk of losing the inn.

Although everyone around her, including the legal advice she'd received, insisted she was not at risk of losing her home, she remembered the pain and loss in Millie's eyes. Maggie feared the woman's need to claim her identity would force Millie to contest Rose's will.

Maggie's breathing returned to normal, and she kept focusing on what she might feel if she were in Millie's shoes. Maggie couldn't imagine her life without her family. Her children meant everything to her and without them, she'd be lost. All Millie wanted was to know for certain that her mother wasn't lying to her, and that she was indeed Robert Lane's daughter, and Maggie couldn't fault Millie for that.

Maggie instinctively knew that Millie didn't care one bit about running the inn. Whatever Millie's plans were they most certainly would include getting money from the sale of the inn and then probably leaving Captiva for good.

However, Maggie didn't believe that money was the driving force behind Millie's legal threat. The only solution would be to give Millie what she wanted more...a family of her own, and that was something Maggie Moretti could give her.

She opened the box once again and took out the plastic bag. Not wanting to disturb anything in it, she kept the rest of the contents together and closed the box, returning it to the corner of the attic. Maggie pulled the light string once more and climbed down the ladder. She pushed the ladder back up and in place and carried the plastic bag to the carriage house.

Tomorrow, she'd go to Millie and give her what she wanted, a chance to belong to something. It was a leap of faith on Maggie's part, and because she didn't want anyone to talk her out of it, she decided to tell no one. That was the biggest risk of all.

———

Maggie's cellphone rang and startled her awake. It was Lauren.

"Hey honey, what's wrong?"

"Are you sitting down?" Lauren asked.

Maggie pushed herself up to rest against the bed's headboard.

"I'm actually lying down. Will that do?"

"I'm sorry, Mom. I know it's early, but I couldn't wait any longer."

Paolo turned to face Maggie. "What's going on?"

Maggie shrugged and wiped the sleep from her eyes. She needed coffee, badly, but there was no time.

"Grandma is selling her house and plans to move to Captiva Island."

That news shocked Maggie awake. "What? She can't do that. I mean, what exactly did she say?"

"I've been dealing with this for the last couple of days. She said she was going to call you, but I thought I'd better get ahead of that and prepare you. She hasn't called, has she?"

"No. I haven't heard from her in about two weeks. I was going to call soon. She'll probably call me today. It's Sunday. She always calls me on Sundays."

"What are you going to say to her?" Lauren asked.

"I'm not sure. I guess the first thing is to get showered, dressed and drink at least one cup of coffee before I talk to her."

"I guess the better question is how would you feel about Grandma living near you?"

Maggie sighed. "I'm not sure how I feel about it. You just hit me with this news. I'll need more time to think about it. The truth is that I don't like being so far from her and I hate having you deal with her all the time. You don't need the added stress, especially with the baby coming and all."

"I don't mind, Mom. She can be difficult, but not so much that I can't handle it. You've got your own troubles down there, Grandma moving to Captiva is going to be one more headache you have to handle."

Maggie laughed. "You know honey, I can't believe I'm saying

this, but your grandmother moving to Captiva is the least of my worries. Anyway, thank you for letting me know. How are you feeling these days?"

"The morning sickness isn't as bad. I'm going into my fourth month and showing. The girls are so excited to be big sisters."

"You still don't want to know the sex of the baby?" Maggie asked.

"Nope. We like to be surprised. We're grateful for a healthy baby and pregnancy. I've got to go. I'm sorry if I woke you, but I doubt you'll be able to get back to sleep after this news."

Maggie laughed at the suggestion.

"You've got that right. You take care honey. I'll let you know how it goes with Grandma."

As soon as Maggie ended the call, Paolo sat up in bed.

"Please tell me that whatever the news is, you're not going to call a Code Red."

Maggie smiled. "It's news all right, but this time I think we can skip the Code Red alarm."

Maggie decided not to wait for her mother to call. She rang her daughter Sarah first.

"Hey, Mom. What's up?"

"I've got news about your grandmother," she answered.

"You mean that she's moving to Captiva? Lauren told me."

"I guess your sister forgot to tell me that. Who else knows?" Maggie asked.

"I think all of us. Well, maybe Beth doesn't know but the rest of us knew two days ago because she's enlisting everyone's help on it. Trevor is even looking into finding her a place down here. I was going to come over to see you today and talk about it. Lauren told me that Grandma was going to call you. I thought she had by now."

Maggie plopped into her chair. "No. She hasn't called me and I think I know the reason why."

"Huh?"

"She's going to get everything in place so it will be hard for me to say no."

"You don't want her here?" Sarah asked.

"It's not that, honey. It's just that your grandmother can be difficult, and I don't want to fight with her."

"Is fighting inevitable? Can't the two of you get along?"

"Yes, of course we can, but things are different now. She's not going to come down here and take over my life. I won't put up with it."

"Then you stand your ground and make sure she knows who's boss right from the start. As soon as she sees that you're in control of your life and your decisions, she'll back off. Trust me, Grandma is going to create a social life down here that you'll be happy about. She needs a life of her own just as you need yours. I think it will be fun to have her around, and her great-grandchildren will be thrilled to have her near."

Maggie smiled at Sarah's words. "I'm sure you're right, honey. If I don't hear from her by the end of the day, I'll give her a call and see what's up. Heaven knows, when your grandmother gets down here, Captiva Island will never be the same."

CHAPTER 18

Chelsea's idea for Ciara to talk to Crawford was a good one. The only problem was that when she approached him, his two sons interrupted and Ciara was put off once again. Crawford's behavior was making Ciara more worried by the day, and she planned to talk to him about it right after speaking with Maggie and Paolo. She'd held off talking to them earlier because she didn't want to worry her brother, but now she was desperate for help.

She drove to the Key Lime Garden Inn and searched for either Maggie or her brother but couldn't locate them. She walked into the kitchen and saw Riley making gnocchi.

"That's a lot of work. I used to make them but I haven't had the time," she said.

"Don't tell anyone this, but I learned a new secret for making them. I'm almost embarrassed to tell you since you were born in Italy and know how to make them yourself," Riley said.

"I'm intrigued. What's your secret?"

"Instant potato flakes," Riley whispered.

"You're kidding me," Ciara said, shocked at the admission.

Riley nodded. "I'm telling you, it's incredible. They make the fluffiest and lightest gnocchi I've ever tasted. You should try it yourself. Just don't tell anyone your secret."

Ciara laughed. "I won't."

Just then, Maggie and Paolo walked into the kitchen.

"Good morning, Ciara. It's good to see you," Maggie said.

Ciara hugged her brother and Maggie. "I hate to bother you guys, but do you both think you could spare a few minutes? I wanted to run something by you."

"Is everything ok?" Paolo asked.

"Yes, of course."

"Sure, why don't we go over to the carriage house?" Maggie said.

"Ciao, Riley. I'll be back to taste the gnocchi when they're done. I can't wait to see how they come out."

"I'll be here," Riley said.

Maggie, Paolo and Ciara walked into the carriage house, and settled into the living room.

"Can I get you something to drink?" Maggie asked.

"No, thanks. I'm good."

"Well, what's going on?" Paolo asked.

Ciara explained what had been going on between her and Crawford lately, and unlike Chelsea, Maggie seemed concerned. Her brother, however, acted like she was making a big deal out of nothing.

"This is the island's busy season. You've lived here long enough to understand what that means. Restaurants, hotels, and especially Powell Water Sports are awfully busy this time of year. He's lucky to have Joshua and Luke helping him. I'm happy for Finn that he's doing what he loves, but since he left to go to flight school, Crawford has had his hands full," Paolo explained.

"I understand all that, but Crawford and I have been dating long enough that I know when he's different, and it's not because of his workload. Something is going on with him and I'm worried that he's rethinking dating me. I know that sounds crazy, but maybe he's concerned that after all this time, I'm expecting an engagement."

"Are you?" Maggie asked.

"I hate to admit it, but I guess I was hoping that by now, he might have proposed. It never occurred to me that I could be sending Crawford subtle signals. Do you really think that's it? Do you think he's feeling pressure from me and is slowing our relationship down?"

So far, Paolo hadn't said a thing and let Maggie do all the talking. Ciara wondered if her brother was uncomfortable talking about such things. It wasn't his way to dig deep into relationships.

"I think it's possible, but the only real way that you're going to know what's going on is to talk to Crawford. We can only assume what he's thinking and I don't think we're helping you much with that. We could be completely off-base."

Ciara was disappointed. She'd come no closer to understanding what was happening with Crawford than when she began talking to Chelsea, Maggie and her brother. They were right of course. Talking to Crawford was the only way to get to the bottom of things, and she wouldn't be put off one minute longer.

"You're right. I'm going to talk to him right now. This can't wait. He's too important to me to leave things hanging in the air like this. Thank you both so much for helping me with this. I've been a wreck for a while now. I'm going over there right now."

She got up and headed to the stairs. "Love you guys."

"We love you too. Let us know how things go," Maggie said.

"I will."

Ciara ran down the stairs to the driveway. She was scared but felt lighter for realizing that whatever happened between her and Crawford, it would be for the best. She'd been true to herself and wouldn't change for anyone, not even for Crawford Powell. If that meant they were about to break up, then so be it. At least she would have fond memories of a time when she felt love, and that was the most important thing of all.

———

Paolo smiled as he watched his sister leave.

"What's got you smiling? You look like the cat who ate the canary," Maggie said.

"Oh, nothing except Crawford came to me three days ago to ask for Ciara's hand in marriage."

Shocked, Maggie looked like she was going to hit him. "And you never said a word to me about it?"

"I was going to but so much has been going on around here, I forgot to mention it."

Maggie beamed. "This is so exciting. I can't wait for Ciara to tell us that she's engaged."

"You should see the ring. I didn't ask but I'd bet it's at least two carats. The thing is huge," he said.

"Two carats isn't huge these days, but I'll tell you, that girl is so in love I don't think she'll care one bit about the size of her ring." Maggie wrapped her arms around her chest. "Oh, I'm so happy for her."

Paolo nodded. "So am I, and Crawford as well. I know Julia would be happy for him. It's been several years since she passed. It's not good to be alone."

"Tell that to Linda St. James. She's had a crush on Crawford for years, especially during the hurricane. He came to her rescue and I swear she saw a knight on a white horse when he did. Wait until she hears that Crawford and Ciara are engaged. I can't wait to see her face."

"That doesn't sound like you, Maggie. You sound as if you want her to suffer," Paolo said.

"Not suffer. You know how Linda is, always acting like she's the island's queen. Every now and then I like to see her knocked down a peg or two. Is that so wrong?"

Paolo smiled. "I'll never understand women."

Maggie laughed. "That's to our advantage."

"How about we have a nice dinner tonight? Why don't we go for a swim and then you get dressed for a night down at the beach? I want to watch the sunset with my wife."

Maggie wrapped her arms around Paolo and kissed him softly on the lips. "I would love nothing more."

"I was just getting ready to call you," Crawford said to Ciara as she entered Powell Water Sports. "What are you doing tonight?"

"Not much, you?"

"I'd like to take you to dinner. We've been so busy around here lately, it's hard for you and me to get some down-time. I'm sorry about that. How about a date night?"

"I'd like that."

Just then Luke came into the room. "No can do tonight, Dad. Joshua isn't feeling well. He thinks he's got a cold. I'm going to need you with me for the sunset cruise."

"Are you kidding me?" Crawford asked.

Luke looked at Ciara. "Any chance you can help out too? Jen said she needs help behind the food counter. It's the worst-case scenario but with her foot in a cast, she's a bit unsteady."

Ciara shrugged. "I guess so, now that my date has just been canceled."

She didn't mind working the sunset cruise. She'd done it before and if it was the only way she could spend time with Crawford, she'd take it. She pointed at him and smiled. "Don't think this is our date. You still owe me a night of romance and dancing."

Crawford laughed. "You got it!"

"I'll see you both later. I've got a few errands to run as soon as I get home."

"Don't forget to be down on the beach at five-thirty. It takes us a bit of time to stock the kitchen and bar."

"I remember. I'll be there," she said. She gave Crawford a kiss on the cheek and walked out of the shop, racing to get herself ready for a night of tourists and music.

When he'd put everything in place, Crawford Powell thought long and hard about how he would propose to Ciara. He was a romantic at heart, and wanted to ask her to marry him in a way that would make the sweetest memory for both of them. Their road to love and commitment was a journey of mutual respect and an acceptance of each other's view of the world.

For Crawford, the loss of his wife to cancer years earlier meant that his focus shifted to his children and the role of being both father and mother to them. The idea of falling in love again never crossed his mind.

Over the years since her death however, Crawford noticed Ciara walking in the neighborhood, and slowly their friendship developed into something more. The balance between independence and togetherness evolved over time, and his children and Ciara's family supported the blending of two families.

He'd been preoccupied and nervous as soon as he picked up Ciara's engagement ring. He was terrified that he'd lose it or that Ciara would find it before he was ready to propose. He could tell that Ciara was confused about his behavior the last two weeks, and so he decided that he needed to move things along quickly by asking Paolo for her hand.

Once that was done, he was ready to propose. He'd put everything in place and the final step was getting Luke to pretend Joshua was sick. Jen had broken her foot, so that part was true, but everything else that he and Luke told Ciara about the sunset cruise was an act.

Tonight, the boat would be theirs alone right after the proposal. Unbeknownst to Ciara, both families would be present on the beach and there would be someone to video the entire celebration.

The boat would be lit with hundreds of lights. Playing in the background, the DJ would be ready as soon as Ciara walked toward the boat.

To pull all of this off, Crawford enlisted the help of Ciara's brother, Paolo, who would keep everything a secret up until the last minute. Earlier in the day he let Chelsea know, so that she would be able to join them, and he had to assume that by now, Maggie knew as well. He even got Luke to set things in place for Becca to watch the proposal on video.

Everything was going according to plan. He only had one more stop to make.

The cemetery was off-island and although Julia's plot and that of her mother and grandmother were cared for by the groundskeeper, Crawford, several times a year, came to pay his respects and add new flowers when needed.

It had been two months since he'd been to the cemetery and although he offered his apologies to his wife for his absence, he knew she would understand. He brought tools and a bucket for the water and cleaned out the dead flowers and weeds before planting the new orange star flowers that Julia loved so much.

When he was finished cleaning all three plots, he returned the tools to the car. He then walked back to Julia's headstone and put one single stone on top. He knelt down and cleared his throat before speaking.

"Hey, honey. I know you've been watching over all of us, and so, what I'm about to say should come as no surprise. I'm getting married again, or at least, I think I am. I haven't asked her yet, but I plan to in a couple of hours."

He looked around to see if anyone was nearby, but he was the only visitor in the area.

"I remember you talking about what you wanted for me after you were gone, but I wouldn't let you. You kept telling me that I needed to have someone in my life and that you didn't want me to be alone. I used to hate it when you said that. I just couldn't imagine my life without you in it, so I couldn't see what you were trying to say."

As hard as he tried, he couldn't stop a single tear from falling. He wiped his cheek and continued.

"I get it now. I understand how a person can be surrounded by so many people and still feel completely alone. That's how it was for me...until Ciara. When she came into my life, I felt like I was reborn in a way. I didn't even know I was dead until her."

He got up from the ground and looked around again just to make sure no one could hear him.

"The kids love her too, so I know that would make you happy."

He smiled, and then added, "Anyway, I wanted to thank you for helping me be a good husband. I remember me teasing you and saying how lucky you were to have me. If I didn't ever tell you, I was the lucky one. I'm who I am now because of you. I just hope I'll be good enough for Ciara."

As always, Crawford wanted to stay but knew he had to leave. Even though he had the most wonderful future waiting for him, it was hard to say goodbye again.

He moved from side to side, feeling awkward and excited at the same time. In the end, he said what he always said before leaving Julia.

"Rest easy my love and keep watch over us all."

CHAPTER 19

he reflection of the twinkling boat lights out on the water and tiki flames along the path to the shore confused Ciara so much that she thought she was at the wrong boat. The sun was another two hours away from setting in the sky, but the lights still illuminated everything.

Ciara soon realized she'd come to the right place when she saw several friends and family lined along the path leading to Crawford.

Ciara's face lit up with a combination of surprise and amusement. Most likely due to his job, Crawford never dressed up but now, to see him in a linen Hawaiian shirt and dress pants shocked her.

"What in the world?" she asked him as he approached. "What is all this? What are we celebrating?"

Crawford answered her by getting down on one knee and opening a small blue box.

"I wanted this to be as special for you as possible. I invited our family and all our friends to be here for this moment. Ciara, I love you with all my heart. Will you marry me?"

Her hand covered her mouth and her eyes filled with tears.

She'd wanted this day to come for so long, and now it was here. She couldn't wait to answer him.

Nodding, she answered, "Yes, I will."

Crawford put the ring on her finger and stood, pulling her to him and kissed her deeply on the lips.

The crowd erupted in cheers and whistles, and although she knew they were surrounding them, she didn't want to move out of his embrace. There would be plenty of hours of celebration but in this moment, she couldn't pull herself away from Crawford's arms. When she finally did, she was astounded by the view. The most important people in her life were present.

Her brother Paolo and Maggie were the first to congratulate them. Paolo hugged his sister and wiped the tears on her face. "Congratulazioni per il tuo fidanzamento, sorella! Sono davvero felice per te."

"Grazie, fratello. Significa molto per me avere il tuo sostegno."

Maggie kissed her cheek. "We're both so happy for you."

"I guess I'm going to have to learn to speak Italian," Crawford said.

"Ah, that's a good idea," Paolo answered. "Everyone should learn to speak Italian. It's a beautiful language."

"Congratulations, Dad," Becca yelled from the large monitor nearby.

Ciara waved at the screen. "I can't believe you guys are here for this." She turned to Crawford. "You really went all out."

"I can't take credit for any of the technology. Joshua took care of it for me."

In another surprise, Crawford's son, Finn, who had traveled from Ft. Lauderdale for the occasion stepped up.

"Finn! I'm so happy you're here."

Finn, Joshua and Luke all kissed Ciara and shook their father's hand.

"Congratulations, Dad, Ciara," Finn said. "I wouldn't have missed this for the world."

Riley carried appetizers to everyone on the beach, Iris directed everyone to take a glass of champagne from the white linen-covered table. Off to the side, the DJ played music to get the crowd dancing right away.

Sarah, Trevor and Chelsea hugged Ciara and Crawford and hovered over Ciara's engagement ring. Even Linda St. James raised her glass of champagne to the couple.

Chelsea didn't feel right leaving her sisters at home, and wanted everyone to meet them, so she introduced Tess, Leah and Gretchen to the group.

"Welcome to Captiva," Ciara said. "I'm glad you could join us."

"We hope you don't mind us crashing your party," Tess said.

"Not at all," Crawford answered. "We're happy to meet Chelsea's family. The more the merrier. How long will you all be visiting the island?"

"Just for a week. We're driving to Key West and thought we'd stop and visit Chelsea and Captiva. It's really beautiful here."

Maggie walked to the computer monitor to spend time with her son and daughter-in-law.

"So, I hear you, Michael and Gabriel have been cornered by your grandmother to help her move down here," Maggie said.

Christopher laughed. "You could say that. She seems in a hurry too. I think this winter really did her in, and then her ankle sprain made things even worse."

"She can hurry all she wants, but...wait, what ankle sprain?" Maggie asked.

"Didn't Grandma tell you? She was in one of her Zumba classes and after she left, her ankle hurt. She went to the doctor, who told her it was a sprain and she should elevate it. She'll be fine."

As frustrated with her mother's latest decisions, Maggie hated that she couldn't stay on top of her mother's medical issues. Nonetheless, she still didn't want her mother to rush down to Florida too soon.

"Well, she can't get down here until we've found her a good place to live. I can't have her staying here. It's too much for me."

"Are you feeling ok, Maggie?" Becca asked.

"Oh, I'm fine. I'm just so busy with the inn and everything. No matter what my mother thinks, I'm not on an extended vacation."

Paolo, Ciara and Crawford joined Maggie.

"We're really so happy that you both could be here for this, honey," Crawford said.

Becca smiled. "Are you kidding? I wouldn't have missed it for the world. Where are my brothers? Get them over here so we can say goodbye."

Crawford waved Finn, Joshua and Luke over to join them.

"Hey Josh, thanks for setting this up. Finn, how many hours have you had flying so far?"

"I'm nearing three hundred. I'm still a baby," he said laughing.

"Are you still seeing Jillian?"

Finn blushed. "Yeah, it's back and forth to where she lives, but it's working out."

"How's medical school?" Luke asked.

Becca rolled her eyes. "Exhausting."

The monitor started to blink in and out and Joshua looked behind it to find the problem.

"Josh, it's ok. We've got to go anyway. Thanks for doing this. Dad and Ciara, we're so happy for the two of you. Make sure you keep us updated on wedding plans. You know we'll be there on your special day."

"We will, honey. We love you both," Crawford answered.

Joshua unplugged the computer and Luke picked up a microphone.

"Hey everyone. Let's raise our glasses to my dad and Ciara," he announced.

Another round of cheers and whistles followed, and Luke continued his speech.

"Thanks everyone for coming out and sharing this special

moment. You should have seen Dad before you got here. He was a nervous wreck."

Everyone laughed at that. "Anyway, because you were here to support them, I think that helped ease his nerves. Please stay on the beach and have a good time, but now, my father and Ciara are getting on this boat and heading out to enjoy the sunset without the rest of us. I think they deserve a little private time, don't you?"

Everyone clapped, and Crawford placed his hand on Ciara's lower back, leading her to the small boat that would take them out to the sunset cruise boat. When they got inside, they waved to the crowd that had run to the edge of the water to say goodbye.

Crawford turned to Ciara and smiled. He had done what he'd set out to do. He had won the heart and love of Ciara Moretti, and whatever more blessings he would receive in his life, nothing would be more precious than that.

CHAPTER 20

Maggie placed the platter of cinnamon buns on the kitchen counter. Her guests loved her scones, but she loved to mix things up and bake something different now and then.

Chelsea appeared at the back door and breathed in the aroma. "What did I tell you?"

"Huh?"

"Didn't I tell you before my sisters arrived that I'd either be in jail for killing them or at your back door early every morning until they leave. Consider this my first escape," Chelsea said.

Maggie chuckled. "Come in and get one of my cinnamon buns. The coffee is ready. Pour me a cup as well, will you? I'm about to call my mother and I can't do it before my first cup or by the time I hang up with her, I'll have a major headache."

"Oh, and here I thought I had it bad. I wouldn't want to be you for the next hour for the world."

Riley seemed amused by their exchange. "I'm glad my mom is on the other side of the country."

"Riley, I didn't know you and your mother had issues, and where is she living these days?"

"California. Issues? I think if you were to ask her, she'd tell you that we get along fine. I'm the one who struggles every time we talk."

"I'm sorry to hear that," Maggie said.

"Don't get me wrong. I love my mother. It's just that whenever we talk she complains that she doesn't have any grandchildren. So far Grace isn't pregnant, and I'm not even seeing anyone. I guess it's a crime to be close to thirty and not at least be engaged."

"It's not a crime, sweetie. The right person will come along and if it's what you want, you'll get married when the time is right for you and not a minute before," Maggie said.

"That's what I say," she answered.

Chelsea ate her cinnamon bun without adding anything to the conversation. Maggie turned to watch her friend devour the bun.

"You've got frosting on your face," Maggie said.

"I'm in heaven, leave me alone."

"I assume that you're running away from home to get away from your sisters, so what's going on?"

Chelsea took a sip of her coffee and one by one licked each finger.

"My sisters are planning to open a business in Key West. They're moving there permanently."

"That's exciting. What kind of business?"

"They're combining their two talents and opening a coffee shop and pet grooming shop. They're going to call it the Key West CoiffeeShop."

Maggie looked at Riley, and then back at Chelsea. "You're kidding, right?"

"Nope. That's the thing about my sisters. I couldn't make this stuff up if I tried. That's not the wildest part though. They want me to invest in their business."

Maggie's eyes widened, "They asked you for money?"

"The day they arrived. They weren't in my house for more than fifteen minutes when they asked me."

"What did you say?

"I told them no. I'm not trying to be a mean sister here. I explained that I'm living on a fixed income and I can't spare the money."

"That seems like a reasonable answer," Maggie said. "They don't seem to be too upset about it. They looked like they were having a great time at Ciara and Crawford's party."

Chelsea shrugged. "So far. We'll see. Anyway, I've got to get back. I promised them that we'd have a nice day on the beach. Tess said they want to get a tan before they get to Key West."

"Sounds like a good time. Maybe I'll join you all later. Right now, I've got to call my mother. Save me a spot on the beach."

Coffee in hand, Maggie walked into the carriage house and up the stairs to call her mother. Her mother answered the phone without a hello or any other cordial greeting.

"I wondered how long before you'd get around to calling me," she said.

"Hello, Mother. I'm fine, how are you?"

"My ankle is killing me and it's cold here. I bet it's hot where you are."

"It's a comfortable eighty-two degrees. I'm sorry your ankle still hurts. Why didn't you tell me that you'd hurt it?"

"You know how I don't like to make a fuss."

Maggie rolled her eyes at that comment. "What did the doctor say?"

"He's a hack. After my doctor died from lung cancer, they gave me this young kid. I don't think he knows what he's doing. I don't like him."

"You don't like him because he's young or something else?"

"You didn't call me to talk about my doctor. Let's get to it. What have you found for me down there?"

Maggie took a deep breath and tried not to lose patience with her mother right off the bat.

"I only found out a couple of days ago that you were planning to move here. We're going to need a bit of time to find the right situation. Did you explain to Lauren what you were looking for?"

"We talked, but that granddaughter of mine wants me in an assisted living place and I'm not ready for that. If I was, I'd just stay here, stay inside and wait to die."

Great. I've been on the phone with her for less than five minutes and she's already trying the guilt trip thing.

Maggie tried again. "Lauren's going to work with Sarah and Trevor on finding you the right situation. I'm sure they'll get you what you want."

"I don't like everyone looking at places without me. I think I should come down there and look at them myself. I'm the one who's going to live there after all. Don't you think I should have a say in where I'm going to spend my money?"

"Of course you'll have a say. They're just saving you time by looking at places and weeding out anything that isn't right. When they've narrowed the selection, then you can look it over. You'll have the final say. Isn't that what you want?"

In her lifetime, finding the exact words to say to her mother that weren't threatening, combative or dismissive had always been an issue for Maggie. Now, in the interest of time, she chose her words carefully so that they could get off the phone without too much friction.

"Yes. I want a final say. That sounds right. What about you?" her mother asked.

Confused, Maggie asked, "What do you mean?"

"I mean, are you going with them to look? I want your opinion too. These kids are young and they don't see things the way you and I do."

Maggie almost spit out her coffee. It surprised her to hear her mother say that they were alike in anything.

"If you want me to get involved, I will," she answered.

"I do. Let the kids do what they will, but when they end up with a few for me to see, you go check them out first. If you don't mind, that is."

"If you feel it will help you, I'm happy to do it," she said.

"Good. Well, I've got to run. I'm preparing for a yard sale next weekend. You have no idea how many things a person can accumulate in fifty years. Do you think there's anything in my attic or the basement that you'd want? I can have the kids put them aside for you."

The last thing Maggie wanted was more junk from her past. "No, but thanks for the offer. I'll call you in a few days and see how you're doing."

The call was the first time that her mother had ever asked for her help. She wondered if there was a lasting change between them or if this was a fleeting moment in her mother's acceptance of her vulnerability.

Whatever it was, Maggie felt a shift in their relationship. However subtle, she could tell that when her mother finally arrived on Captiva Island, she would need Maggie in ways she never had before. If her new role was to be a caregiver, she accepted it wholeheartedly, and prayed that she'd find the strength and wisdom to deal with whatever came next.

CHAPTER 21

*M*ost of the afternoon, Maggie researched what it meant to use DNA to prove paternity. There was so much involved and she was certain that without a definitive test result, Millie wouldn't be able to move forward.

Chelsea knew it too, and Maggie understood that it was the reason her friend didn't want her to keep any of Robert Lane's possessions. However, there were several issues with what Maggie assumed was Robert's hairbrush. First, she couldn't be certain that it was his. It rested on Robert's dresser along with his wallet, watch and comb, so logically she assumed it was his, but there was no guarantee.

From what she'd learned from her research, the hair follicles in the brush must have a root to be a viable sample. She looked at the hairs again but couldn't tell if there was a root. Even using a magnifying glass didn't help. What she did notice was that there were many more hairs than she first noticed.

Accuracy percentage on such tests were low, but the hairbrush was all she had…all she could offer Millie, and none of it would help her gain control of the inn. Maggie was more certain of that as the days passed.

She put the plastic bag inside another bag to conceal it and, without telling anyone, got in her car and drove to Millie's. She kept watch on the clock in the car. It would be easy to explain a short trip off-island to go shopping, but not if she stayed out too long. She had no idea if Millie would be home, but she took a chance and reached her home within forty-five minutes.

Walking to the front door, she took a deep breath and knocked. When Millie answered the door, she didn't smile.

"You're back," she said. "Do I need to call a cop?"

"I'm sorry about the other day. Can I come in?" Maggie asked.

Millie hesitated, but then opened her door wider so that Maggie could enter.

"I don't know what else there is to say. It seems we both said what we needed the last time you were here."

"I know it seems that way, but I've had some time to think about your situation."

Millie seemed irritated. "My situation?"

"Your search for your biological father," Maggie answered.

"You don't have any right to talk to me about that. As a matter of fact, I've never said anything to you about searching for anyone. My mother made it clear. My father is Robert Lane."

Maggie carefully chose her words but needed to say what she'd come here to say. "You don't know that for certain."

"Are you saying that my mother lied to me?" Millie asked.

"Are you certain enough to think you'd win a legal battle for the Key Lime Garden Inn?"

Maggie knew she'd hit a nerve with her words.

"Millie, please listen to me. I support your desire to find out the truth. If Robert Lane is your father, then so be it. The only way you might get the answers you want would be through DNA testing. I've done some research on this. It's not one hundred percent accurate so I'm not sure it would hold up in a court of law, but it might make you feel better."

Confused, Millie pointed to her sofa. "Maybe we should sit."

Maggie's heart jumped in her chest believing she was making progress as they moved to the sofa.

"Would you like something to drink? I don't have much...a couple of cans of sparkling water."

"That would be nice," Maggie answered.

Millie went to the kitchen as Maggie thought about how to explain the DNA testing.

When Millie returned to the living room with the can, she asked Maggie, "So, how exactly would that work?"

"My understanding is that it's not possible to get anything from his body. He's been gone too long, and his son the same. What I found online was other possible objects that could provide viable DNA to test. One place takes hair follicles from a hairbrush. Although the accuracy rate is not good, something around sixty percent."

Maggie could see disappointment in Millie's face, and wanted to give her hope but there was little to be had.

She handed Millie the plastic bag with Robert's hairbrush inside. "We believe this to be Robert Lane's hairbrush, but again, we can't be sure about that either. You can have it and send it to the lab if you want to pursue this further."

Millie took the bag and looked inside.

Maggie warned, "You shouldn't disturb the brush too much."

Millie gently closed the bag.

"If there are hair follicles with a root, the lab can use it. I have your email address so I can forward everything I've learned about the lab and the test. You'd have to mail it to them as they're not near Fort Myers, but there may be other labs closer. It's up to you."

Millie hugged the bag close to her body. "How much does the test cost?"

"It varies, but probably around three hundred dollars. You'll need to investigate the best place for your needs, but that's the amount I've seen."

Millie nodded. "Why are you doing this for me? I don't understand," she asked.

Maggie smiled. "You and the rest of my family I would guess, but I have my reasons. Nothing means more to me than my family. I've been through a lot these last years and there is no way I could have gotten through it all without them. I realize that your mother is gone and if Robert is indeed your father, you don't have him either. I'm so sorry about that. To be honest, if he is your father, I think it was awful that he didn't acknowledge it when he was alive, but it isn't my place to pass judgment on that."

Millie smiled for the first time since the day Maggie hired her to be bookkeeper at the Key Lime Garden Inn. "I feel the same way, but there's little I can do about that now I guess."

Maggie placed her hand on Millie's arm. "Family comes in all sorts of shapes, sizes and configurations. Relationships and connections we make as we live our lives can provide just as much, and sometimes even more, support, understanding, compassion and love. The answers you're looking for may be in the past, but I think there's a good chance that they're in your present. When you look at things that way you might see a different future than the one you've imagined thus far."

Maggie got up from the sofa and left the can of water on the coffee table.

"I've got to get back. If you want to let me know how you're making out with the test, or anything else for that matter, you know how to reach me."

Millie walked her to the door.

"Thank you for this, Maggie. I'll be in touch."

"You're welcome. I hope things work out the way you want."

Maggie smiled, thinking that this time she wasn't being pulled out of the building by Chelsea. This time she was gently escorted to the door.

Maggie's ride back to Captiva was slow due to the traffic getting over the Sanibel bridge. She was content that she'd accomplished what she set out to do and hoped that only good things would come of it. Regardless of Millie's next move, Maggie could look herself in the mirror and know that she stayed true to her beliefs. Millie was sixty-three years old and had already struggled so much in her life. In Maggie's opinion, no one, not even Millie, deserved to feel so alone for the rest of her life.

When Maggie finally reached the inn, Paolo and Chelsea were on the back porch to greet her.

"We've got news!" Paolo announced waving a piece of paper in the air.

Maggie had already decided to tell her family that she'd been to Millie's and was ready to explain the minute she saw Paolo.

"Me too," she said, "but you two look like you're going to burst, so you go first."

"Robert Lane never owned the Key Lime Garden Inn. The property was built in the 1930s by the Johnson family...Rose's family. When she married Robert, they were still going back and forth from Connecticut every year, but the Connecticut house was in her family's name as well. Rose sold that years ago and put it in a trust for their son. The Johnson family was pretty wealthy, but Robert Lane didn't have two nickels to his name back then, and over the years, Rose never put his name on the deed. She was one, smart lady," Paolo said.

Maggie grabbed the document from him. She looked over the paper, her eyes wide.

"Where did you get this?" she asked.

"Chelsea suggested I look into the history of the property which is public record at the Town Hall," Paolo said.

"To be honest with you, Mags, I just woke up one morning and thought about your situation. There was so much unknown, I thought maybe Paolo and I could go to the Town Hall and see if there were any clues as to ownership."

Maggie was speechless.

"Why we didn't figure this out earlier, I don't know. I mean we all just assumed that Robert's name was on the deed. I remember Rose telling me that it was her family who came to the island when she was a kid, but I never put two and two together."

"Chelsea and I got to thinking that maybe we missed something that was right under our noses from the start," Paolo explained.

Maggie sat on the porch swing, the paper clutched in her hand, and started to cry.

"Oh geez, this I didn't see coming," Chelsea said sarcastically.

Maggie shook her head, and answered through tears, "I'm fine. I think it's just tension being released."

Paolo sat next to her on the swing and put his arms around her.

"When Rose sold this place to me, I remember thinking there was no way I was up to the task of taking care of this place and dealing with Sanibellia. But then you came along. You are the reason the inn exists today. You brought it back to life. The Key Lime Garden Inn is you Maggie. All of it and will forever be in your family."

She looked at Paolo and patted his hand. "Our family."

The three of them stayed on the porch for some time, talking about Rose, the history of the inn, and what the future might look like.

"Wait. You said you had news too. What is it?" Chelsea asked.

Maggie smiled and looked at her friend. "Today was a good day, Chelsea, a very good day."

CHAPTER 22

*A*fter Maggie explained what she'd done that morning, she felt relieved with the combined positive progress in their lives. Paolo and Chelsea agreed that it was a good thing Maggie didn't tell them about her plans before she went to Millie's because they would have tried to talk her out of it.

Presenting them with a fait accompli meant there was nothing more to do but support Maggie's choice. By all accounts, they agreed her going was a good thing.

"Where are your sisters?" Maggie asked.

"I left them on the beach again. Apparently, they're not dark enough."

Maggie jumped up off the porch swing. "I'm getting my swimsuit on. I haven't had five minutes to enjoy the beach in weeks. Not to mention I'm exhausted from cleaning all the rooms and doing laundry. If I never see another bedsheet again, I'll be in heaven."

"I can't believe you haven't filled the housekeeping position yet," Chelsea said.

"I know, and it doesn't help that this is one of the busiest seasons we've ever had. Give me a few minutes and we'll walk down to the beach together."

Paolo kissed Maggie's cheek. "I'm headed back to the garden. I'll see you at dinner. You ladies have a nice relaxing afternoon."

Maggie carried her beach bag and Tommy Bahama chair and followed Chelsea to the beach. Because Chelsea's sisters were sitting on the stretch of beach near Chelsea's house, they walked down the driveway and out onto the street to get there. Tess and Leah were in the water and Gretchen was laying on her lounge chair.

"Hey, Maggie. Are you joining us or just stopping by?" Gretchen asked.

"Nope, I've brought my chair and plan to sit on it until someone drags me off this sand. Not even rain will make me budge. I need my beach time as much as possible. I guess you could call it my drug of choice. How are you and your sisters enjoying Captiva?" Maggie asked.

"This island is Paradise. We've really enjoyed being here, and it's got us excited about Key West too. Living in Florida will be so much more relaxing than living up north, and no more snow," Gretchen answered."

"The only time I miss the snow is during the holidays. We do our best to decorate a palm tree or two, but it's not the same," Maggie said.

Tess and Leah joined them and grabbed their towels. "Hey Maggie. Nice to see you again," Tess said.

"I'm thrilled to finally have time to enjoy this weather," Maggie answered.

"We've got iced tea and homemade lemonade, Maggie, if you want some," Chelsea said.

"Sure. I'll take a lemonade."

Chelsea filled a plastic cup for Maggie and saw someone waving from the corner of her eye. As the woman approached, Chelsea realized who it was. "Oh, no. I can't believe it."

"What?" Maggie asked.

"Isabelle Barlowe. She's coming over here."

Isabelle was fully dressed in her Carolina Herrera dress, stiletto heels, and carrying a Birkin handbag on her arm. Running in the sand with no thought to how ridiculous she looked, she reached the women and waved.

"I'm so glad I found you ladies. I just left the inn and Paolo told me you all were down this way."

She looked at Tess, Leah and Gretchen and smiled. "Hello, I'm Isabelle Barlowe. I'm friends of Chelsea and Maggie. My husband, Sebastian and I live in North Captiva, and you are?"

"Isabelle, these are my sisters who have come for a visit. This is Tess, Leah and Gretchen."

"How lovely. How long will you be visiting Captiva?" Isabelle asked.

"We're getting back on the road next Sunday," Tess answered.

"On the road? Where to?"

"Key West, we're moving there," Gretchen said.

"Oh, Chelsea, how wonderful that your sisters will be nearby."

Maggie laughed. "Not so close actually. It's about a seven-hour drive. It's over four hours by plane."

Confused, Isabelle asked, "But it's in the same state, am I correct?"

"Yes. But Florida is a big state," Chelsea answered.

Everyone smiled, and Chelsea explained. "Isabelle moved to Captiva from France last year so she's unfamiliar with Florida."

Isabelle clapped her hands together. "Well if this isn't fortuitous. I was coming to invite you to my home for a get-together. It's been forever since we've had you over. Now we have an even better reason for having a party." She looked at Chelsea and then at Maggie. "You must come. I'll be offended if you don't."

Chelsea's sisters' faces lit up and Maggie tried not to laugh. She knew exactly what Chelsea was thinking. Her sisters needed money, and Isabelle Barlowe had more than she could ever spend in one lifetime.

Fortuitous, indeed.

"We'd love to," Leah said. "Thank you so much for the invitation."

"Well, I must go. I have a million things to do this afternoon." Turning to Chelsea, she said, "Let's say seven o'clock on Friday night?"

Chelsea smiled and nodded. "We'll be there."

Isabelle left and Chelsea looked at Maggie and rolled her eyes. If she could, sometime before Friday she'd do her best to come up with a good reason why they couldn't make it. Keeping her sisters away from the Barlowes was a good idea. Chelsea was sure that Isabelle would thank her later.

The next morning, Paolo drove Maggie to her appointment at the hospital. It was four months since her last radiation and now it was time for her to have scans to see if the cancer had returned.

Chelsea's sisters spent hours trying to get the perfect tan. But as much as Maggie loved the sun on her skin, she protected her body from too much sun by sitting under the umbrella that Chelsea had outside her place. The fear of any kind of cancer, including skin cancer, kept Maggie vigilant about caring for her health.

She made green smoothies often and took vitamins, which was something she never did before the cancer diagnosis. She'd been looking into meditation and focused on her breathing. Soon she'd be adding yoga to her schedule and Zumba class with Chelsea.

However, nothing meant as much to her or soothed her spirit the way her early morning walks along the beach did. She didn't need bright sun to enjoy those quiet moments. She preferred days that were cloudy, hazy or had a bit of fog or mist. On those days, she felt more connected to herself and the world around her.

The waves perpetually hitting the shore, the salt air, the seashells collected, all reminded her that it didn't matter whether she controlled anything in her life. The sun would rise and set regardless of what she thought about it, and that gave her more contentment than anything else.

She left Paolo in the waiting room and followed the nurse to the back corner of the first floor. Walking down hallways and through automatic doors after the nurse pushed a button, Maggie felt at peace with her appointment. She didn't worry about the cancer returning. It would happen or not regardless of what she thought about it.

And so, she decided to think about Chelsea, her sisters and the upcoming party at Isabelle's, and do her best for the next thirty minutes not to giggle uncontrollably.

CHAPTER 23

Sarah pulled books off the shelf and put them into a box. It was a slow process because every book she removed she'd read the first few pages. Sarah had already told Ciara that she was quitting, and it surprised her that Ciara had been expecting it all along. In fact, she told Sarah that she'd wondered what took her so long to admit that the balance of family life and work, at least for now, was too much for her.

Ciara walked into Sarah's office carrying two cups of coffee. "I thought maybe you could use this," she said.

"Thank you so much. You're a lifesaver. I was just about to go get a cup."

Sarah got up off the floor and took the cup to her desk.

"I know you've got work to do but take a break and keep me company."

"You're going to need help getting these boxes out to your car," Ciara said.

Sarah nodded. "I know. Trevor is coming at noon to help me carry them out to the car."

"So, bittersweet leaving?" Ciara asked.

Sarah sighed. "It is. I'm going to miss everyone here, but I know it's the right thing to do. Noah is getting into swimming now, which is something I have to keep an eye on because of his seizures."

"Has he had more?"

"Not for a few months, and it was very mild, nothing like when he was younger. They expect that he will outgrow them, and so, that's what we're hoping. Our nanny has been great, but it's a burden that I'd rather her not take on by herself."

"It sounds like you're doing the right thing. I've often wondered how you managed with three kids."

Sarah laughed. "By the skin of my teeth, that's how. So, tell me, how does it feel to be an engaged woman? Any wedding plans you'd like to share?"

Ciara shook her head. "Not yet. As far as how I'm feeling now that I'm engaged? You tell me...are my feet touching the ground? I feel as if I'm walking on clouds every day."

"Aww, that's so sweet. Crawford is a great guy. I'm really happy for you both."

"Thanks. One thing I told him that I want is to take him to the village in Italy where I grew up. Gaeta is a beautiful place. He says that he'd love to go, so that's the plan right now. Besides, there is so much more to see in Italy. He's never been there and I'm the perfect person to introduce the country to him."

"How awkward will it be running into Maurizio though?"

Ciara shrugged. "I don't think he'll be there. He left Gaeta and moved to Rome. He got a job and met a woman, so it wouldn't surprise me if he's already married."

"How do you know all this?" Sarah asked.

"Every so often he sends me an email telling me about his life. It's so funny because he can't stop apologizing for his behavior when he was here. He ends every single email with an apology."

Sarah laughed. "Oh, poor Maurizio."

Sarah looked over at the bookcase and then back at Ciara. "I can't put it off any longer. I better get back to packing up. Thanks for the coffee. Promise you'll stop by before noon to say goodbye?"

They stood up and Ciara hugged her. "You know I will. Thank heaven that you and I are friends outside of work. I couldn't bear it if I was never going to see you again."

"I feel the very same way," Sarah answered. "I'm not sure I ever thanked you for this, but Trevor and I are together because of you. If I hadn't come here that day to help with the Food Pantry, I might not have ever met him."

Ciara laughed. "I remember how much you hated him that day."

Sarah smiled. "I thought he was so obnoxious, but I couldn't take my eyes off of him. Now we're married with three children. Who would have ever predicted this?"

Ciara put her arm around Sarah. "Me, that's who."

Brea had a new routine. She'd get to class just as it was about to start and not a minute before. If she was lucky, she could get a seat in the front row, if not she'd make the best of it. As soon as the class was over, she'd walk as fast as she could out the door and to her car.

She stopped going to the campus coffee shop and instead would pick up her coffee at the Starbucks drive-through on her way home.

While in class, she kept her focus on the professor and her eyes straight to the front of the class. Whatever she had to do to avoid Hudson Porter, she'd do.

He seemed a nice enough man, but he constantly singled her out before class to talk to her, and it made her feel uneasy. She feared she'd appear rude, but there was no other way to avoid the awkwardness between them.

Frustrated that the class she enjoyed the most was fraught

with anxiety and frayed nerves, she considered quitting the class altogether. Her frustration turned to anger and she vowed not to let Hudson bother her.

She walked into her creative writing class and saw that Hudson wasn't in his usual seat. Looking around the room, she couldn't find him anywhere. It was the first time he'd been absent from class, and also the first time Brea felt relief. She enjoyed the class much more thanks to his absence and even went to the campus coffee shop when class was over.

However, when she got close to her car, she could see Hudson leaning on it. Her heart raced with worry that he wasn't just another student sharing writing ideas with her before class. Hudson Porter was, in Brea's mind, a genuine stalker.

"Hey, Brea. Sorry I missed you earlier. I had something important at work I couldn't get out of. I guess that's the downside to being an older student...lots of other responsibilities."

"I've got to get home, Hudson so I don't have any time to talk," she said.

"Oh, of course. I'll be brief. I just wanted to ask you if you'd be interested in going out one night for a drink or dinner. Whatever you'd like."

She couldn't believe that he was asking her for a date. She was certain that she'd mentioned her husband and children.

"I'm married, Hudson."

He chuckled. "So what? So am I," he answered.

Brea wasn't sure why his words shocked her so much, but her reaction surprised her as much as it did Hudson. She formed a fist and punched him square in the face.

His hand went to his nose, and he seemed genuinely shocked. "What was that for?"

"For being a sleaze. Go ahead and press charges if you want. I'm sure your wife would love to hear about what you've been up to. And, if I forgot to mention this before, my husband is a cop."

She moved closer to her car to open the door, and Hudson

flinched and backed away, obviously worried that she'd slug him one more time.

Brea smirked at his reaction and how brave she was. In the past she would have run home to Michael to have him handle the situation. But these days, she was feeling more empowered than ever before. She just never thought she'd have to defend herself by punching someone in the nose.

Smiling, she drove home thinking about her creative writing class. Maybe Hudson would be there, but maybe not. Either way, she was going to enjoy her class more now than ever before.

"How much would you pay me for that?" Grandma Sarah asked her neighbor.

"Five dollars?" he asked.

"Sold!" she said, grinning from ear to ear.

"Grandma," Beth whispered, "I thought you loved that bowl."

"I did once. Let it go to someone else's house," she answered as she leaned on her cane, going back into her garage to get another bowl.

Beth looked at Lauren and asked, "Have you ever seen her like this? She used to hold onto everything. I remember trying to throw out an old disgusting sponge and she told me I was being wasteful."

"Something is going on with her. I'm not sure what it is but she's been acting strange the last month." Lauren shrugged. "I guess all we can do is keep an eye on her. Sarah and Mom are going to look for a place for her near Captiva. I expect they'll find something in Sanibel."

Beth nodded. "Yea, I've looked at the homes for sale on Captiva and there isn't much at all."

"Have you talked to Mom since you've been back from your honeymoon?" Lauren asked.

"No, we came directly to Becca and Chris' because of the yard sale. We're staying overnight tonight and then will drive home in the morning. I'm going to call her later tonight."

Beth rubbed Lauren's belly. "How is my little niece or nephew doing?"

"Not much activity yet, just a flutter every now and then," Lauren said.

"Can someone give me a hand with this?" Grandma yelled as she tried to lift her sewing machine table.

"Grandma don't try to pick that up," Beth said as she and Gabriel ran to help.

They placed the table on the grass and Grandma went directly to an unsuspecting bargain hunter and started her sales pitch. "This sewing machine table is an antique. They get a lot of money for these things you know."

The woman wasn't interested and walked away.

Grandma made a face at her as she did and Beth and Lauren giggled.

"I hope Mom knows what she's getting into having Grandma live near her," Lauren said.

"Well, one thing's for sure. Mom won't stand a chance if Grandma joins forces with Chelsea. Can you picture the two of them hanging out?" Beth said.

"They already are," Lauren said.

"Huh?"

"They're doing virtual Zumba together. Well, they were before Grandma hurt her ankle. My guess is as soon as she's feeling better, they'll go to Zumba somewhere down there. I think Grandma said that Mom was going to join them. Can you picture it?"

Beth laughed and shook her head. "I cannot, but then again I never would have imagined that Grandma would move to Florida. I guess anything is possible with this family."

Lauren rubbed her belly. "You can say that again."

CHAPTER 24

*M*aggie checked out her guest and then went upstairs to clean the bedroom. She pulled the sheets and pillow cases off the bed, gathered the dirty bath towels from the bathroom floor, and threw away the used soaps and emptied the trash. The flowers and water in the vase needed changing, and although the inn had central air conditioning, she opened the windows while she was cleaning just to get a few minutes of fresh air to circulate around the room.

The other bedrooms were not only full of guests, but they also all were still sleeping, even though the kitchen smells were inviting. Her guests were on vacation and it was their prerogative to sleep as long as they wished. As far as Maggie was concerned, the longer the better because it would give her more time to enjoy her morning routines.

She'd had her early morning walk, made a pot of tea for herself instead of coffee, and spent quiet time in her special room surrounded by Rose Johnson Lane's journals, and a few of her own.

Rose's room had become Maggie's and she treasured the times when she could sit and look out at the butterfly bush which was filled with blue and yellow butterflies. It was where she kept Rose's memory alive. The walls of the room were covered in photographs from the past and a few new ones of Maggie's children.

She'd changed her cellphone ringtones to match her children's telephone numbers. Sarah had taken Maggie's phone and together they selected songs for each of her siblings. The only problem was that Maggie couldn't remember who was who and found that when her phone rang she had no idea who was calling without looking at her phone.

When her phone rang Over the Rainbow, she looked at it and saw that it was Beth.

"Hey, honey. Are you home yet?"

"Yes. We got home the day before yesterday but drove to Chris and Becca's instead of going home. Grandma had her yard sale yesterday, so we wanted to be there to help. We're back at our house now."

"That was nice of you. How did it go?"

"She sold almost everything she put out and what she didn't sell got taken away for free at the end of the yard sale. I think she made about five hundred dollars."

"Wow, that's impressive," Maggie said.

"You should have seen her, Mom. She was a regular sales woman. She instinctively seemed to know exactly what kind of pressure to put on people. One minute someone was looking at something, put it down, and then Grandma swooped in and made the person change their mind. She'd make the sale, take their money and move on to the next victim…I mean shopper."

Maggie laughed at the image. She put her journal down, stretched her legs out and onto the ottoman and leaned back to relax as she listened to her daughter tell story after story about the yard sale and their Hawaiian honeymoon.

"Mom, have you ever been to any of the Hawaiian islands?"

"Nope. I always wanted to go, but somehow we never got

there. Your dad and I were always content to travel down here or go camping with you kids now and then."

"Oh, you and Paolo have to go. It's incredible. Oahu is my favorite island although we haven't seen all of them. We plan to check them out in the future. I can't wait to go back. Oahu is so lush with tropical forests and mountains. You drive through what looks like a hidden Paradise and the next thing you know, you're inside a mountain. It rains all the time for a little bit, but then the sun comes out. One day…"

Maggie could hear Beth talking but as she looked at the photograph across from her chair, something caught her eye. She'd looked at this picture what seemed like a thousand times, but she'd never looked close until Millie recognized her mother in the photo.

"Beth, everything sounds wonderful. One of these days, Paolo and I will travel to Hawaii. It's on my bucket list for sure. I've got to go now, though. I've got so much to do today. Isabelle Barlowe is having a party tonight for Chelsea's sisters who are visiting."

"That sounds like fun. Don't work too hard, ok?" Beth said.

"I won't. Love you, honey. Say hello to Gabriel for me."

"Will do. Bye, Mom."

"Bye, honey."

Maggie opened her desk drawer and found a magnifying glass. She pulled the framed image off the wall and moved to the window for better light. Examining the photo closer, she wondered what to make of what she had found.

The photo was of the entire staff of the Key Lime Garden Inn, back when Millie's mother worked as a housekeeper. As Millie had pointed out before, her mother stood as close to Robert Lane as she could. Everyone was facing the photographer. Everyone except one young man who was staring directly at Millie's mother.

Maggie didn't know why it intrigued her so, but she wanted to know who the young man was. She dialed Ciara's cellphone.

"Hey, Maggie. It's nice to hear from you. What's up?"

"Do you remember what we ended up doing with all those old bookkeeping books? Did we keep them?"

"Yes, we kept them. Paolo packed them into a plastic storage bin. I'm not sure where he stored the bin though. I have to assume it's in the attic somewhere."

"Thank you. I'm looking for information on past employees of the inn. I'm pretty sure wages and information of the people who worked here were inside those books."

"They are. I saw that myself. I'm grateful we do everything on the computer now, but I think they were well organized for the times," Ciara said.

"Thank you, Ciara. I'll check with Paolo. Have you and Crawford decided when the wedding will be?"

"Not yet. We're still talking about it," she answered.

"Well, I hope you both know that you are always welcome to have it here if you want."

"That's very kind of you, Maggie. I'm sure that's what my brother would want, but we haven't decided yet. I'll talk to Crawford and let you know. Let me know if you need my help with those ledgers. Will we see you at the Barlowes' tonight?"

"Yes, I've got to get ready," Maggie said.

"Me too. I'll see you then."

Maggie hung up and then called Paolo at Sanibellia.

"I know. I know. You want me to come home so we can get ready for Isabelle and Sebastian's party. I'm leaving now," he said .

"No, it's not about that, although, yes, it's getting late. I'm calling because I wonder if you remember what we did with those old ledgers and bookkeeping journals of Rose's. Ciara said you put them in plastic bins but I don't remember seeing them in the attic."

"I put them in the bins so they'd stay dry. They're in the eaves part of the attic. I stacked several of those things there because I didn't think we'd be needing them anytime soon. Why?"

125

"Oh, I was just curious. I wanted to make sure we still had them. There's something I want to check out," she answered.

"Not tonight I hope," he said.

"Heaven's no. I don't want to cut it too close. I'm getting in the shower now. I'll see you when you get home."

"Ciao, Bella," Paolo said.

Chelsea and her sisters were not the first to arrive at the Barlowes'. There were several men and women who Chelsea didn't know, and she wondered if they were new friends or people Sebastian never introduced to her when they were dating.

Isabelle met Chelsea at the door and Sebastian followed behind in his wheelchair.

"Sebastian, these beautiful women are Chelsea's sisters. This is Tess, Leah and Gretchen. Ladies, this is my husband, Sebastian."

"Welcome to our home," he said. "It's lovely to see you again, Chelsea."

"Thank you for inviting us," she answered.

Maggie, Paolo, Ciara and Crawford arrived are the same time and came into the foyer to join everyone.

Isabelle kissed Maggie and then directed everyone outside onto their veranda overlooking the ocean.

"What a marvelous home you have," Gretchen said, admiring the view.

Two waiters carried champagne and hors d'oeuvres of prosciutto-wrapped asparagus, shrimp cocktail, and beef tartare on crostini to every guest.

Not knowing anyone at the party, Tess and Leah and Gretchen stayed close to Chelsea and did their best to engage with others, but Chelsea could tell that her sisters felt uncomfortable and awkward.

Isabelle stood behind her husband and put her hand on his shoulder. "Sebastian, Chelsea's sisters are driving to Key West in a few days. They plan to live there."

"Is that so? I've been to Key West several times. It was years ago of course but I remember having a wonderful time. I think you ladies will love living there, so much activity and beautiful nature. Do you have plans once you arrive?" Sebastian asked.

"Yes, we hope to open a business there. It will take a little time but we're hopeful," Gretchen answered. "It's a combination store actually. We're opening a coffee shop that will also be a pet grooming store. Tess and Leah have had experience in those two fields for many years now. We plan to call it The CoiffeeShop."

"What a perfect name. It is French, no?" Isabelle asked.

Chelsea chuckled. "I don't think they thought of that when they came up with the name, but as it happens, yes, I suppose you're right."

"But, of course. Coif is a French word. It means to fix the hair...to cut and style. This is incredible. Do you already have a location picked out for this shop?"

Tess and Leah perked up and began to ramble on.

"No, not exactly. There are a few possibilities but we need to get there and find just the right place," Tess said.

"Yes, we have a lot of work still to do, but we're hopeful that we'll find something. Of course it will take a lot of money. Key West can be expensive. We hope to see if the bank will help us. We're hard workers and will make a success of it," Leah added.

"We hope the bank will see it that way and lend us the money," Tess said, her eyes wide with anticipation.

Chelsea wanted the floor to swallow her up.

In her excitement, Isabelle insisted that it was fate that brought Chelsea's sisters to Captiva. How else would they have known that Sebastian's wife was French?

"Sebastian, we must invest in this business," Isabelle announced.

Sebastian looked at Chelsea who couldn't say much in front of her sisters.

"What do you think, Chelsea?" he asked.

Maggie overheard the conversation, and quickly moved to stand by her friend.

"I'm not really the one to ask, Sebastian. I mean, my sisters' business is their own. I can vouch for their work ethic."

It was the closest thing to a compliment that Chelsea could muster for her sisters, but she couldn't bring herself to recommend her friends give money to them. She hated being put in such an awkward position, but the minute Isabelle invited them to their home, Chelsea saw the train wreck approaching.

"Consider it done," Sebastian said.

Tess and Leah practically jumped up and down, and Gretchen smiled and thanked them for their generosity.

"Come into my office and I will write you a check," he said.

Isabelle clapped her hands together and watched as Tess, Leah and Gretchen followed his wheelchair into another room.

Maggie put her arm around Chelsea who looked at Maggie and shook her head. "How many more days until they're gone?"

"Four," Maggie answered.

"I'm not sure I can make it," Chelsea said.

"What was it that you said to me about dealing with Millie? I'll carry you until you can."

"Yeah, but there's a difference. You weren't going to kill her."

CHAPTER 25

"*H*ow could you all do that?" Chelsea asked at breakfast the next morning.

"What did we do?" Tess asked.

"You practically begged my friends for money. I'm so embarrassed I don't have words," Chelsea responded with more than a tinge of anger in her voice.

""I beg to differ. It seems like you've got words all right," Gretchen added. "And we didn't beg."

"Chelsea, Isabelle was genuinely excited," Leah said.

"Yeah, especially when she heard the name of our new business," Tess said.

"How much money did they invest?" Chelsea asked.

"Twenty-five thousand," Gretchen said.

Chelsea grimaced.

"Don't be angry at us for that. We never asked for any particular amount," Tess added.

"What difference does that make? These are my friends and it looks like I set them up for you to take advantage of them and the situation. Can't you see that?"

"The situation?" Tess asked.

"The fact that they threw a party just for you all. I'm sure had they known that their guests were grifters, they wouldn't have let you come within ten feet of their property," Chelsea argued.

"Grifters? You're calling us grifters?" Gretchen asked. "I've never been so insulted in my entire life."

Chelsea rolled her eyes. "Oh, please. Why do I think that's not true?" She reached for her car keys and purse, and looking at Gretchen, said, "Give me the check."

"I will do no such thing," Gretchen responded.

"I'm not asking, I'm telling you to give me that check. It's going back to the Barlowes this instant," Chelsea insisted.

Leah tried to calm the situation. "Chelsea, I understand how you feel, but please trust us, we never tried to con your friends out of their money. It was an honest offer that we accepted graciously. Please don't make this worse than it already is."

Chelsea's heart pounded in her chest. She was furious, but Leah, who had always been the peacemaker in the family, pleaded with her to let it go.

"Fine, but this changes nothing. I'm still disappointed in all three of you."

Chelsea stormed out of the house and got in her car, headed for the Barlowe estate. She was on the road for two minutes when she received a call from Maggie.

"What are you doing?" Maggie asked.

"I'm trying not to hit people with my car, you?"

"Why in the world are you driving with that attitude?"

"Maggie, sometimes it's better to not know the answer to such things. What's up?"

"Since you're already driving, can you come over here?" Maggie asked.

"I can if you can give me about an hour. I'm headed over to Sebastian's. I need to apologize for my conniving and manipulative sisters."

"Oh, now I understand. Well, just try to calm down by the

time you get here because I need you to help me with something and I'd appreciate it if you weren't in a bad mood."

"I can't promise anything, but I'll do my best. I'll get there as soon as I can."

Chelsea couldn't imagine how she might calm down after the exchange with her sisters. The more she thought about their behavior, the angrier she got. When she reached the Barlowes', she got out of the car, pulled her pencil skirt down and took a deep breath.

Her apology was only one reason for her visit. If she could, she'd try to get them to cancel their check. Her sisters were not going to get away with scamming her friends, if she had anything to say about it.

"My goodness, Chelsea. This is an honor. This makes three times this week we've seen each other."

"Hello, Isabelle. I'm sorry to bother you and Sebastian this early, but I wonder if I might come in and talk with you both for a minute."

"Of course, please come in. Sebastian! Chelsea is here," Isabelle yelled.

"Can I get you anything?"

"No. Thank you. I can't stay long. I just wanted to speak with you and Sebastian about…"

Sebastian wheeled out to join them. "Hello, Chelsea. We had a wonderful time last night. Your sisters are delightful."

"Yes, well, that's what…I mean, who I wanted to talk to you about. I really appreciate what you did for them, writing that check and all. It was too generous. You really shouldn't have, and I don't think you would have had you not been coerced by my sisters."

"Coerced? I don't feel that way. Isabelle and I are very happy to help. We're glad to do it."

"I understand that, but, you see, there is every possibility that their business will fail and you'll lose your investment. It isn't fair to do that to you. You would never have been in that position if it weren't for me and our friendship. I'm asking you to please cancel that check. Let's keep our friendship just that and not involve business transactions."

Sebastian's laugh was a deep roar and Chelsea couldn't understand what was so funny.

"Chelsea, my dear friend. Do you have any idea how much money I have lost over my lifetime? Some investments are successful and some others not. Twenty-five thousand dollars is nothing if it helps your sisters, and if I lose it, then c'est la vie."

Isabelle put her arm around Chelsea's waist.

"It's true, Chelsea. Sebastian and I only want the best for our friends. We don't think of this money so much as an investment but rather a gift. If we make the money back, then wonderful, but if not…well, it will be fine."

Chelsea didn't know what to make of their gesture, but there was little she could do to change anyone's mind. She stayed a few more minutes and listened to their stories about the party the night before.

She'd been so angry that she hardly paid much attention to anyone or anything after her sisters' shameless behavior, and Sebastian and Isabelle were kind to overlook her preoccupation. Despite her friends' benevolence, Chelsea remained ashamed of her sisters, and she expected that feeling to persist for a long time.

Maggie met Chelsea in the driveway. As soon as her friend got out of her car, Maggie grabbed her arm and pulled her toward the inn.

"Come with me," Maggie ordered Chelsea. "And why are you so dressed up?"

"I'm not dressed up, I'm just out of my pajamas at nine o'clock, something you're not used to seeing."

Chelsea was right. Maggie couldn't count the number of times her best friend came for breakfast wearing her pajamas or loungewear, and a few times she even walked to the inn from her house still wearing her slippers.

They went to Maggie's office where Paolo was standing in front of a table with the plastic bin filled with the old bookkeeping ledgers.

"Hey, Chelsea. Thanks for coming," he said.

"What's going on?"

Maggie handed Chelsea the photograph that had Millie's mother in it. "This is what's going on." Maggie pointed to the young man in the picture. "Do you see that guy there?"

"Yeah, who is he?" Chelsea asked.

"That's what we're trying to find out," Paolo said.

Just then, Ciara came in through the front door.

"Ciara, we're in the office," Paolo called out.

"Hey, everyone. What's happening?"

"Ciara, remember I asked you about these old bookkeeping ledgers?"

Ciara nodded. "Yes, I remember."

"Well, we're trying to figure out who the guy in the photo is. The one who isn't looking at the camera. Is there any way, based on the photo and the payroll entries, that we can figure it out?"

"Not from that photo, but there is another book that had individual employee photos. I remember seeing them," she said.

Ciara searched inside the bin found an envelope stuffed into the back of a book with the employee photos that Maggie was looking for. "Here they are."

All four of them looked at the photos and tried to match the larger picture with the smaller ones.

Holding up one photo, Maggie said. "This one. Isn't this him?"

"That's him. What's his name?" Paolo asked.

"Ralph Hanley. He was a bus boy. He lived in Fort Myers. It says here that he was seventeen years old...just a baby," Maggie said.

Ciara nodded. "He'd be eighty years old now."

"That's if he's still alive," Chelsea added. "Why do you care about this kid, anyway?"

Maggie once again held up the framed picture and handed Chelsea her magnifying glass. "Look at this photo again. Who is he looking at?"

Chelsea looked into the glass and then smiled. "Millie's mother, Kathleen. Do you think...?"

"I think it's worth pursuing for a DNA test. We just have to find out if he's still alive," Maggie said.

Paolo shrugged. "Let's hope he still lives nearby. I don't mind following up with this, but I'd hate to think we'd have to travel far to get our answers."

Maggie nodded. "For our sake and Millie's."

"How about this? Let's get Sarah involved as well. She and Ciara are the best at online research. Let's see if we can find this guy as fast as we can."

Ciara nodded. "I'll call Sarah and have her come over here. It's better if we work out of this location. Who knows what else we might find that will require rummaging through these books and documents for more clues."

Maggie smiled and hugged Paolo. "Let's all say a prayer that we've found Millie's biological father."

"And that she'll be as excited about it as we are," Chelsea said.

CHAPTER 26

*M*illie decided against the lawsuit, so when Attorney Doyle contacted her, she told him that she'd changed her mind. He tried to get her to at least come back to his office to discuss the case.

She reminded him that there was no case and to please stop calling her. The one thousand dollars that she'd received from the pawn shop remained in her wallet and she did everything she could to not spend much of it at all. But, she had to eat, and in a week she'd be out on the street, unable to pay the rent on the lovely home she rented for the last couple of months.

There wasn't any point in pursuing the lawsuit, and from the research she'd done and with Maggie's advice, she saw little reason to send the hairbrush for DNA testing. She couldn't depend on the accuracy of the test, and the truth was that, even if she could prove that Robert Lane was her father, it would take a lot more money and time to contest his will. In the end, she decided to believe her mother, think of herself as Robert's daughter and move on.

With everything that had happened in the last two weeks, the one thing Millie hadn't counted on was Maggie's kindness, and she wondered if she could impose on her once more. Millie desperately needed a job and one that paid well. But with everything that she'd put the Moretti family through, she couldn't expect that they would welcome her back with open arms.

Still, her stubborn pride would keep her poor and alone if she didn't at least try. And so, she decided that she would drive to the Key Lime Garden Inn, apologize and ask for her job back. She prayed that the job hadn't already been filled, and that Maggie could forgive her. Money was not the only reason she wanted to work at the inn. She would be content having a connection to her mother and father while living each day with gratitude for her life and hope for her future.

Millie filled her gas tank only halfway. It was more than enough to get to the Key Lime Garden Inn and still save her money. These days she didn't drive often, leaving the car in the driveway and only taking it out for absolute necessities. Depending on the Sanibel Bridge traffic, she might get to the inn in less than an hour. As she drove to Captiva Island, she prayed that everything would go as planned, and in a few hours, she could feel the weight of her financial burdens lifted. She'd be able to plan, to save and most importantly, pay her rent.

A couple sat on the back porch enjoying their breakfast, while another sat on the porch swing drinking coffee. She didn't see Maggie or Paolo anywhere and decided to walk to the front of the inn and go inside through the front door.

No one was at the check-in desk, so she walked past it and into the kitchen. Riley and Iris were busy preparing food for the day and seemed surprised to see Millie standing in the doorway.

"Millie," said Riley without smiling. "What are you doing here?"

"I'm looking for Maggie. Is she here?"

Riley came from behind the kitchen island and stood in front of Millie, blocking her from coming inside further.

"Maggie and Paolo had to run an errand. They might not be back until tonight. What do you want?"

Millie could tell that she wasn't welcome, and it made her feel awful. She didn't blame the entire staff for feeling this way. It was her fault that everyone, including the chefs, knew of her threatening behavior.

"Maggie and I talked. She came to my place the other day. I wanted to thank her again and run something by her."

It might have been sneaky, but it was Millie's only way to explain to Riley that she and Maggie were at least on speaking terms.

"You shouldn't be here, Millie," Iris added. "We'll tell Maggie you were here, but you should go now."

Millie looked at Iris and then at Riley and realized there was no point in trying to change their minds. "Please let her know that I was here and ask her to call my cellphone as soon as she can. Thank you."

Frustrated that she'd wasted gas and time by driving to Captiva, she admonished herself for not calling first. She got back in her car and drove to the parking lot. With no idea of how long Maggie would be gone, she decided to park hour-by-hour and stay on the island until Maggie returned.

She got out of her car and walked to the beach. Walking to the edge of the water, Millie took off her and felt the soft sand under her feet. It was early enough that the sand was still cool and almost cold where shade covered the ground.

She carried her shoes and headed toward the Mucky Duck and beyond. Imagining herself living in one of the homes along the beach, she wondered when they were constructed. Back when her mother worked at the Key Lime Garden Inn, she'd taken photos with her Polaroid camera. None of the majestic homes were in those photos. Most of what she saw on Andy

Rosse Lane didn't exist during her mother's time on the island, and Millie thought it must have been a big deal to have a job working for such a wealthy family on Captiva.

Millie had no idea how her mother got the job in the first place. The answer to that question and hundreds more that Millie never asked intrigued her. If she was lucky enough to get her job back, she'd research as much as she could about the history of the island and the Key Lime Garden Inn.

She considered herself a Legacy, and suddenly felt immense pride in that fact. It connected her to something bigger than herself, and because of that she vowed not to focus on what she'd lost but what she'd gained in that knowledge.

***

Maggie, Chelsea and Paolo had already contacted two other Ralph Hanleys in Fort Myers with no success. There were several in Tampa, two in Naples and several more on the east coast.

"This is going to take forever," Maggie lamented. "How in the world are we going to find him?"

"Patience, my love. We'll find him," Paolo said.

Sitting in the back seat, Chelsea checked off the last person they called.

Now in Naples, they called the first Ralph Hanley on the list and since no one answered the phone, Paolo suggested they drive to the address.

"This is it, number twenty-six," Maggie said. "Don't park in the driveway, just pull up in front."

Paolo stopped the car just before the mailbox and turned off the ignition.

"Who's going up to the door?" Chelsea asked.

Maggie turned to look at Chelsea. "All three of us. I think

there really is strength in numbers. I think that if he sees all of us, he'll believe it's something important."

"Either that or he'll panic and slam the door in our faces," Chelsea said.

"I doubt it. He's eighty years old. We'll be lucky if he even comes to the door," Paolo added.

They got out of the car and walked up to the front door. Maggie rang the doorbell and a woman came to the door.

"Hello, we're looking for Ralph Hanley. We tried to call but no one answered the phone. We've already called several Ralph Hanleys in Fort Myers with no luck in finding the right man. We may have the wrong Ralph Hanley. Can you help us?" Maggie asked.

The woman smiled and seemed unfazed by three strangers at her front door.

"My father is…Ralph Hanley. He passed away last year. This is our family home. I don't know if he is who you're looking for."

Maggie immediately felt defeated. "I'm sorry for your loss. Do you mind answering a few questions? I promise they aren't very personal but if you could, you'd eliminate your father and we can continue on our search."

"I don't mind. Why don't you come inside," she said. "My name is Kathleen Hannagan."

"We really are sorry to intrude like this," Maggie said.

"It's no problem. What are your questions?"

Maggie pulled out the employee photograph of Ralph. "Can you tell if this was your father? The photo is of a seventeen-year old young man who worked at the Key Lime Garden Inn on Captiva Island. We realize he's very young, but perhaps…"

"That's my father. I know this because he got married to my mother when he was twenty…not much older than this photo. He told us about his time working at the inn and how wonderful the owners were to him. You see, my grandparents died when my father was fifteen years old. The Johnson family took him in and sort of adopted him. They were wonderful people to our family for many years."

Maggie's heart skipped in her chest. They had found Ralph. She pulled out the inn's employee group picture. "Do you recognize your father in this picture?"

Kathleen laughed. "Oh my goodness. I've never seen this photograph before." She brought the picture up close to her face and pointed. "Look! You see that woman?" she asked.

"You mean the one he's looking at?" Chelsea asked.

Kathleen nodded. "I bet she's my namesake. Do you know who she is? Is her name Kathleen by any chance?"

Maggie couldn't believe their luck.

"It is. Her name is Kathleen O'Hara. She was a housekeeper at the inn the same time your father worked there. Why do you call her your namesake?"

"Mom told me that Dad had a girlfriend before her. She told me all about Kathleen and how he was crazy about her."

"What happened? Did she say why they didn't stay together?" Maggie asked.

"To hear Dad tell it, Elvis Presley came back from Germany after spending two years in the military. Dad was so crazy about Elvis—we have all his original albums—that he enlisted in the army just to follow in his footsteps. Of course once he was in the military, he had very little control over where they sent him, but he was happy doing the very thing Elvis did and that was enough for him. He met my mother in 1963 and got married the next year. I was born in 1965. He never forgot Kathleen though. I think it bothered my mother."

"Is your mother still alive?" Chelsea asked.

Kathleen shook her head. "No. Unfortunately, Mom passed away two years before Dad. She had pancreatic cancer. I think Dad died of a broken heart."

"Kathleen, this might be completely off-base, but we think it's possible that Kathleen O'Hara and your father had a child. We're not certain about this, and it's the reason that we've come here today," Chelsea said.

"That's right," Maggie said. "A friend of ours might be that child. She doesn't even know about any of this. We're putting two and two together and want to tell her about our suspicions. We needed to come to see you first."

Maggie, Chelsea and Paolo couldn't say anything more until Kathleen understood what they had presented to her.

Kathleen smiled and shrugged. "I'm actually not surprised to hear this. My father and I weren't very close, and he wasn't the type of man to divulge his deepest feelings with anyone but my mother. The two of them were a real love story, but as I said, he never forgot Kathleen."

"I'm sure your father and mother loved each other very much," Maggie said.

"I can tell you this, though," Kathleen added. "If my father thought that he had fathered a child with Kathleen, he would have married her. Not just out of obligation, but because he truly loved her. I have to assume that he went into the service not knowing anything about a child."

Maggie nodded. "I agree. But now, this child is sixty-three years old and desperately needs to know who her father was. The only way we can be sure is with a DNA lab test," Paolo explained.

"Absolutely. I'd love to know if I had a sister. You're here for my DNA, am I right?" Kathleen asked.

"Well, we weren't even sure what we'd find when we got here. We thought Ralph might possibly still be alive. Are you willing to share your DNA to see if you and our friend are related?" Maggie asked.

"You bet I am," Kathleen said. "When can we do it?"

They all laughed, and Maggie placed her hand on Kathleen's arm.

"Ok, slow down. First, we need to talk to our friend to bring her up to date on what we've found thus far. I'm pretty certain that she'll be just as excited as you are about finding family. She's alone in the world, and I think this will brighten her spirits."

"I'd be very happy to meet her, and I truly hope that we're a match. I'm an only child myself. I've always wanted a sister. I know we're so much older now, but it's not too late. We've still got a lot of living to do. I know my children and grandchildren will welcome a new family member…and Aunt."

Maggie got up from her chair and the rest followed her. They all walked to the door and Maggie shook Kathleen's hand. "I'm so happy that we've met. We'll be in touch just as soon as we can to talk about next steps."

"Thank you so much for doing this. You certainly are very good friends for extending yourself this way. I hope your friend appreciates it."

Maggie smiled. *I hope so, too.*

CHAPTER 27

*M*aggie, Paolo and Chelsea all agreed that Maggie should be the one to tell Millie about Ralph Hanley. They were careful not to divulge Millie's name to Kathleen. It was, after all not their place to assume Millie wanted to meet Kathleen Hannagan. Maggie didn't know exactly how to break the news to her, but with Millie it was always best to be honest and direct.

When her cellphone rang with the *Build Me Up Buttercup* song she knew that Sarah was calling.

"Hey, sweetie. I was going to call you tonight. Grandma wants me to have the final say before she looks at anything."

"That's why I'm calling. Trevor thinks we should look at two retirement communities in Fort Myers. He thinks Grandma would be perfect for them. Both of them are a stone's throw from the Sanibel Bridge. We need to check out Marina Bluff Estates and Sunset Harbor Springs."

"I've driven by both of those places and always wondered what they were about. Are they assisted living facilities?"

"I guess you could call them that but they're even better

because they have properties for all phases of elderly living. I don't think they call themselves assisted living," Sarah answered.

"Good, because if your grandmother hears those words, she'll go through the roof and say she doesn't want to live with, and I quote, "those old people".

Sarah laughed. "I've been looking at both these places online. Trevor was right to pick them. He knows Grandma and understands what we're up against."

"I trust Trevor's judgment. If he thinks they're good, then I'm happy. I'd love to check them out. When can we go?"

"Here's the thing, Mom. These communities are so exclusive you can't just show up. I have to make an appointment for someone to meet us and take us around the place to check it out. Trevor said to let him know when and he'll watch the kids for me. They only show the place on the weekends."

"Well, that narrows my choices. How about this Saturday?"

"The day after tomorrow?"

"That's the one," Maggie answered.

"Great. I'll make the appointments and we can go see them. It's probably best to see them on the same day so everything will be fresh in our minds to compare. I'll text you the times. I'll pick you up on Saturday and drive us there."

"Sounds like a plan. Thanks, honey. Listen, do you think Grandma will have any problem getting in? I mean, exactly how exclusive are these places?"

"You have a point. I don't know enough about them, but in my opinion if they're that snobby, we won't want Grandma living there anyway."

"Good point. I'm almost home. I'm exhausted. I've been running around all morning, and now all I want to do is sit and relax for a few hours. I might even take a nap."

"That sounds exciting," Sarah teased.

"Trust me, Sarah, my darling. It is."

Maggie threw her large tote bag on top of the kitchen table and plopped into a chair. She put her feet up on another chair and closed her eyes.

"I'm not trying to ignore you, Riley. I'm just so tired that it hurts to use my eyes," Maggie said.

Riley chuckled. "You've been crazy busy for the last two weeks. You deserve some down time. Why don't you go next door and take a nap."

"You've read my mind. I think I'll do exactly that," Maggie responded.

Maggie was about to get up from the table when Riley stopped her.

"Oh, no. I'm sorry, but you can't take that nap after all."

Maggie's eyes were wide open now. "I can't?"

"No. You had a visitor. Millicent Brenner was here."

Maggie sat up and put her feet on the floor. "Here? When?"

Riley looked at the wall clock. "About an hour ago. I told her that you were out and most likely wouldn't be back until the end of the day. I told her to leave."

Maggie sighed. "It's all right, Riley. Millie and I have been getting along lately. We're starting to see eye-to-eye on a few things."

"I didn't know. Of course it's none of my business, but can you really trust her?" Riley asked.

Maggie nodded. "I believe I can."

Smiling, Maggie could see that Riley was skeptical. "Did Millie leave a message?"

"Oh, right, she wants you to call her cellphone."

Maggie grabbed her tote bag and quickly dialed Millie's number and waited.

"Maggie, hi. Are you home? Riley said you wouldn't be back until later today."

"Yes, I know, but my meeting ended early enough for me to get back here sooner than I'd planned. Where are you?"

"Sitting on a picnic bench at The Mucky Duck. Do you have time to talk or should I drive home?"

"I've got time. Please, come over to the inn and we'll have lunch. Unless you've already eaten at the Mucky Duck."

"No. I just had something to drink. Lunch would be great. I'll see you shortly."

Maggie hung up and smiled. Suddenly her aches, pains and exhaustion were gone and she had renewed energy. She'd made another decision that she hadn't run by anyone. The Key Lime Garden Inn needed a permanent bookkeeper and housekeeper, and Millie needed a job. Maggie went into her office and found the company checkbook. She smiled knowing that she was doing the right thing.

She came back into the kitchen. "Riley, what's for lunch?"

"Tarragon chicken salad with beets, and I still have plenty of that lemon-orange chiffon cake from last night."

"Perfect. Can you set up for me in the gazebo?"

"How many settings?"

"Just two. I've invited Millie Brenner for lunch."

Millie was suddenly nervous to see Maggie again. She had no reason to fear a confrontation but asking for her job back combined with having to explain how broke she was, made Millie feel more vulnerable than ever before.

She retrieved her car from the parking lot and drove up to the Key Lime Garden Inn, parking her car at the end of the inn's driveway.

She was about to go up the back stairs to the kitchen, when she heard Maggie call her name from the gazebo.

"Over here, I thought we'd enjoy the beautiful day and have our lunch under the gazebo. Have a seat," Maggie said.

"Thank you. It is lovely here. It's the place I saw you for the first time if I'm not mistaken," Millie answered.

Maggie nodded her head. "You're right. You came up out of nowhere and asked me for a job."

Millie smiled. "You were so kind. You didn't mind that I didn't have an appointment and you hired me on the spot."

"Well, as I remember I told you that you were overqualified for the job of housekeeper."

Riley and Iris interrupted and carried platters of the tarragon chicken salad and iced tea.

"Sorry to interrupt, but lunch is served," Riley announced.

"This looks delicious. As usual, you two outdid yourselves." Looking at Millie she whispered, "I've been told that there is a lemon-orange chiffon cake for dessert."

Millie smiled. She hadn't had a dessert like that in quite a while.

Maggie put her fork down and looked at Millie. "Millie, there is something I need to tell you."

She pulled the framed picture that had been in her office out of her tote bag and showed it to Millie. "Do you remember this picture?"

Millie nodded. "I do. My mother is in this photo."

"That's right," Maggie said. "The other day, I was sitting in my office and talking to my daughter Beth. When I leaned back in my chair, I was facing this picture. Beth had just returned from her honeymoon and was telling me about Hawaii when I noticed something in this photograph that I'd never noticed before."

"I don't understand. It's just a group photo. I think it's of everyone who worked here."

"Yes. Do you see this young man here? While everyone else is looking into the camera, this man is not."

Millie's face went white and she realized what Maggie had

seen. "He's looking at my mother. I was so enthralled with seeing my mother and Robert Lane in the picture, I paid no attention to anyone else."

Millie looked up at Maggie. "Who is he?"

"His name is Ralph Hanley. He was your mother's boyfriend at the time."

It didn't register right away, but as Maggie continued to explain about Ralph's daughter in Naples, Florida, everything was becoming clear to her. When Maggie stopped talking, Millie could only ask one question. "So, my mother lied to me?"

Maggie sat back in her chair. "We won't know that until, and that's if, you wish to do a DNA test with Kathleen Hannagan."

Millie's head was swimming with questions. Shocked at the prospect of having a sister who lived nearby was overwhelming.

"What should I do?" Millie asked. It was a silly question because she already knew what she wanted to do.

"I can't answer that. Only you can. I know what I'd do if it were me in this situation. I'd be taking the DNA test just as soon as I possibly could. You could go to a genetic testing lab to get your results, but even Ancestry online has a test you can take that isn't expensive. Once you get the kit, you follow the instructions and then send in the test. I think you will get your results in only a few days."

"Has Kathleen done hers already?" Millie asked. "I don't know, but that's something you can ask her. You'd both have to take the test of course. I think it's the easiest and fastest way to find out. I'm thinking of doing it myself."

What do you think? Do you want to meet Kathleen and the two of you find out if you're sisters?"

Millie nodded. "I think I do. What's she like?"

"She's very nice, and I can tell you one other thing that I noticed right away. She looks like you. You both have the same color eyes, and her voice sounds so much like you that if I were talking to her on the phone, I would mistake her for you."

Millie was overjoyed at the prospect of having a family. In her excitement, she forgot the reason she'd come to Captiva to see Maggie.

"Maggie, I'm embarrassed to say that I'm broke. I don't have much money left and I can't pay my rent. I pawned my mother's engagement ring for one thousand dollars. I came to see you today because I need to ask you to consider re-hiring me as your housekeeper and bookkeeper. I know it sounds ridiculous after what I've put you and your family through these last couple of weeks. I'm truly sorry. Do you think there is any way that you'd consider taking me back?"

Maggie reached inside her tote bag once more and pulled out an envelope. "This is for you," she said.

Millie opened the envelope and found a check made out to her in the amount of three thousand dollars.

"Three thousand dollars? What is this for?"

"It's your paid vacation money. You've been out for a couple of weeks and so, I've decided to continue to pay you while you were out. You'll get back to work first thing Monday morning, right?"

Millie wanted to cry; she was so moved. "I'll be here."

Maggie patted Millie's hand. "Good. Now let's finish our lunch, have that delicious lemon-orange chiffon cake, and you go get your mother's ring back."

Millie didn't hold back her tears. In one day, she had gained so much family that she didn't know what to do with so many blessings. She very possibly had a biological sister, but even if Kathleen wasn't a match, Millie had found family in being an employee at the Key Lime Garden Inn. She'd only wished that her mother could have felt what she felt in this moment...that she belonged.

CHAPTER 28

"Grandma, the banana bread candle is supposed to make your house smell like you've been baking. It's a warm and inviting smell."

Grandma Sarah had been irritated with Lauren moving things around and fussing over her personal decorative choices for the last two days.

"Listen to me, Missy. You practically grew up in this house. You played in every one of these rooms and as I remember it, you sat in this very kitchen and made so much of a mess with cookie frostings and tiny colorful sprinkles that I was vacuuming them up months after you were here. Now, you don't like the way my house looks and smells?"

"It's called staging, Grandma. It's not about what I liked when I was a child or what you like now. It's about appealing to the buyers. Trust me. Selling properties is what I do. It's what I know."

"Well. I suppose so. It just seems to me that if you want my house to smell like I've just baked banana bread, I should be in the kitchen baking banana bread. How are you going to offer the buyers some of the bread? They can't eat a candle."

Lauren sighed and counted to ten under her breath.

"Where did this blanket come from? I didn't buy this."

"It's one of my props. It's just until the house sells."

Lauren didn't know how many more days of her grandmother's complaining she could stand.

"Knock, knock," Michael yelled out as he, Brea and their children came through the front door. "Hey, Grandma, we've come to take you to lunch," he announced.

"Hello dear, I didn't know you were coming. I don't think I can go. There are people coming to look at the house. It's an Open House from eleven to two and then again from three to five." She looked at Lauren. "Lauren, don't I need to be here when the people come?"

"No, Grandma. It's actually better for owners to not be here when people are going through their homes. I'll be fine handling it myself. The less people the better."

Grandma Sarah shrugged. "All right. If you think you can handle it alone, I'll go get my jacket and we can go, but I'll have my cellphone with me. You call the minute someone makes an offer."

"I promise that I will call you. You go have lunch with Michael and Brea and I'll see you later this afternoon after it's all over."

Lauren mouthed a silent thank you to her brother and sister-in-law, kissed her nieces and nephew and walked everyone to the door.

As soon as they were gone, she went into the bathroom, brushed her hair and put on another layer of lipstick. Before long, cars would line up outside and then walk through the home that had so many memories for her. It was bittersweet to watch her grandmother move into the next phase of her life. Lauren would do all she could in Massachusetts to make the transition a smooth one and pray that her mother would soon not struggle too hard to do the same on Captiva Island.

———

When Michael suggested they take Grandma out for lunch so that she wouldn't be around for the Open House, Brea wasn't so sure it was a good idea.

"Can't Becca and Christopher take her?"

"What's the problem?"

Brea shrugged. "Sometimes I worry that your grandmother's negativity will rub off on the kids. She complains constantly."

"I think by now our girls have their great-grandmother's number. Even Quinn goes out of her way to cheer her up every time she complains. Quinn thinks Grandma is just in a bad mood, she doesn't realize that mood has nothing to do with it."

Michael came behind Brea as she was changing Jackson's diaper and hugged her. "It's only for a few hours. Lauren really needs our help."

Brea nodded. She knew it was the right thing to do. She hoped Michael was right about the kids and hoped that they'd remember Grandma's loving and kind words more than the complaints and negativity.

"Let's go! Everyone in the car," Michael said.

"I want to sit next to Grandma," Cora announced.

"You both can do that at the restaurant. Let Grandma have the window."

"How come Jackson always gets a window?" Cora asked.

"Really, Cora? You know the answer to that. He's too little and still needs his car seat."

Quinn laughed.

"What's so funny?" Cora asked.

"You're what's so funny. You're just starting trouble."

"That's enough you two," Grandma said. "As long as I'm in the car, you will behave like two proper young ladies."

Quinn shook her head and Cora just stared at her Grandmother. Brea gave Michael an I-told-you-so look, and Michael just smiled.

The restaurant was twenty minutes away. It was a popular spot for Brea's family whenever they went out to eat, which was no more than twice a month.

The hostess grabbed several menus and everyone followed her to a large round table toward the back. "Do you need a high-chair?" she asked.

"Yes, please," Brea answered.

When everyone was settled in their seats, Brea handed Quinn and Cora coloring paper and crayons that the restaurant provided.

"I think I'll pass, thanks," Quinn said with a tone of maturity. Her twelfth birthday was right around the corner and she was already thinking of herself as a teenager.

Grandma grabbed Quinn's paper and crayons and began coloring in the image. "I suppose you think you're too old for crayons? Good, the more for me."

Brea couldn't make out the look Quinn gave her grandmother but it seemed a mix of confusion and impatience.

The waitress came and took everyone's order. As usual, Quinn and Cora only wanted macaroni and cheese.

"Well, Grandma, you must be getting excited to move near Mom."

Grandma looked up from her coloring. "I'm looking forward to not having to deal with the snow every year, that's for sure." She then softened her tone. "I am looking forward to seeing your mother again...Sarah and her family too."

"I miss Noah, Sophia and little Maggie," Cora said looking at Brea. "Can we go to Florida and see them?"

"I suppose we can, but it will have to wait until our schedules aren't so busy."

"Don't get so busy that I never see you all," Grandma added. "How's that school of yours going?"

Brea's face lit up. "It's wonderful. I'm learning so much. I love everything about it."

"When do you get your report card?" Cora asked.

Brea laughed. "It's not called a report card when you're in college. Remember when I had mid-terms a few months ago? I got good grades on those and then at the end of the school year, I'll have something called finals. I get graded on those too."

"You really don't know anything," Quinn said.

Insulted, Cora came right back with an answer. "I know lots of things, more than you," she said.

Their food came and a quiet fell over the table as they all started in on their plates. After a few minutes, Michael spoke up.

"Well, I have an announcement," he said.

Everyone looked at him in anticipation.

"I'm going back out on patrol, starting Monday," he said.

Brea put her fork down and could barely swallow her food.

"Whose idea was that?" she asked.

"Mine. I've been behind a desk for the better part of a year and I'm miserable. I haven't said anything to you because I didn't want you to get upset but I have to do this. I went into the police force for this very reason. I want to actively be out there doing what I do best...protecting people."

Brea was furious. Michael could have told her this news at any other time but he picked a public place, in front of their children and his grandmother to announce the very thing she'd been dreading for months.

She couldn't react with her honest opinion. She was stuck having to appear pleased and accepting, and even though her face appeared calm, her body reverberated with anger and fear.

"Congratulations, Michael. I'm so happy to hear this. I know your mother will be thrilled too. We've got to call her tonight," Grandma said.

Quinn and Cora only knew that their father was happy and

that their grandmother seemed equally excited. They had no idea that their mother was terrified and unable to say so.

"That's really cool, Dad," Quinn said.

"Yes, you'll have to call your mother tonight. I'm sure that she'll be just as excited about it as I am," Brea said with just a hint of sarcasm.

Several times over the past year Brea and her mother-in-law had talked about the day when Michael would go back out on the street. Neither woman wanted it, and Maggie was just as scared about the possibility as Brea was.

Brea's response to her husband was the only way to convey what she was thinking. She could tell by the look on Michael's face that he got the message, and it was never said but definitely implied that she'd get her chance to say exactly what was on her mind before the day was done.

Grandma's phone buzzed and she could see that it was Lauren calling.

Excited, Lauren said, "Hey, Grandma, I know this is crazy, but there have been two couples who came in, walked around the house and then made an offer before they left. I can't remember anyone ever doing that before, and today it's already happened twice."

"My goodness. What did they offer?"

"Well, they both offered asking price, but when they find out there is a bidding war, I expect the offers to go up. Anyone who is willing to make an offer so quickly wants the house very much. The Open House has only started so who knows what the rest of the day will bring."

"That's great news. I'll let the others know. By the way, Michael just told us that he's going back to his old job. Isn't that great?"

There was a pause on the other end of the line. "Lauren...are you there?"

"Yes, Grandma, I'm still here. Does Mom know?"

"No, not yet. He's going to call her tonight to tell her. Anyway, we're still at the restaurant so I've got to go before my food gets cold. Call me if you have more news."

"I will, Grandma. Tell Michael that I'll talk to him later."

"Will do. Bye."

Grandma ended the call and looked at Michael. "Lauren says that she'll talk to you later."

Grandma went back to eating her lunch, and Brea glared at Michael knowing that, except for his children and grandmother, the rest of the Wheeler women would have a thing or two to say to Michael. Still angry, Brea was glad for their support, but knew that they'd have to get behind her to tell Michael exactly what they thought of his news, and it wasn't to congratulate him.

CHAPTER 29

Sarah picked Maggie up on Saturday morning and they headed for the first of two retirement homes. Maggie had passed Marina Bluff Estates often on her way to the Tanger Outlets near McGregor Boulevard and had heard wonderful things about the place.

"You know I have kept this place in the back of my mind for a possible future place to live if I ever need dedicated care in my old age," Maggie said.

"Seriously, Mom? Do you really think that your children wouldn't be around to care for you?" Sarah asked.

"Honey, I wouldn't want my kids to have to take care of me. My mother is the same way. I know she wants to be closer to me even if she doesn't come right out and say it. But she's still independent enough to resist my hovering over her day-to-day."

"I think when people get old, if they can do it, it's great to be near family that can make decisions for you. That's the biggest problem I've seen working at the Outreach Center. It's the elderly with no one to check in on them and make sure they live their final years with dignity."

A guard station at the entry to the retirement community greeted them as they entered.

"Hello, we're here to see Alissa Mayer," Maggie said.

The guard looked at the papers on his clipboard.

"Drive straight until you get to the white fence. You'll see the entrance to the main building in front of you but go left into the parking lot and then walk up to the walkway. Alissa will meet you there."

"Thank you," Maggie said.

"This place reminds me of Disney. Everything looks so perfect and clean," Sarah said.

Flowers and palm trees adorned the walkway and welcomed Maggie and Sarah with color and light.

Alissa was at the front door as they walked toward it. "Welcome to Marina Bluff Estates," she said.

"Thank you so much. I'm Maggie Moretti and this is my daughter Sarah Hutchins."

"Lovely to meet you. Why don't we go into my office first so I can get a better idea of what you're looking for? We have eight hundred acres here, so we'll be driving throughout to look at options after we talk. Can I get you anything? We have coffee, tea and an assortment of cold drinks as well."

Maggie and Sarah shook their heads. "No, thank you, we're fine."

They entered Alissa's office and instead of Alissa sitting behind a desk, they sat in chairs in the corner of the room.

Looking at Maggie, she asked, "So, as I understand it, you are looking for a property for your mother?"

"Yes, she is selling her home in Massachusetts and will be moving to Florida. She's very independent and drives herself everywhere. She travels and is pretty much still running her own show. Of course, at seventy-eight, that won't always be the case and I can see that she's resolved to find a situation to meet her needs in the coming years."

Alissa laughed. "She sounds like my grandmother. She has her own home here but we're about to move her into something smaller and with more medical care."

Alissa handed Maggie a package with many photos of the different residential properties from which to choose.

"Marina Bluff Estates is a continuing-care retirement community. We have twenty-seven thousand residents living here and thirteen-hundred employees. Each level of care is designed to meet the needs of our residents through independent living, assisted living, and skilled nursing. It sounds like your mother would need something in the independent living section of the estates."

Maggie nodded. "That sounds right."

"It looks like your amenities are extensive, " Sarah added.

"I'm glad you noticed that," Alissa answered. "We have seven restaurants, on-site banking, on-site pharmacy, an eighteen-hole championship golf course, and we schedule several events throughout the year such as concerts and lectures of prominent educators from around the world."

"Wow, too bad you have to be over sixty years old. I'd like to live here," Sarah said.

"Why don't we take a drive throughout the property and we'll spend extra time looking at two homes that are available now."

"Sounds great," Maggie answered.

They toured the rest of the property and then made their way over to Sunset Harbor Springs. Both places seemed perfect for Maggie's mother.

"I don't think we could go wrong with either of these places, what do you think?" Maggie asked Sarah.

"I agree. Ultimately, it will be Grandma who will make the final decision. Do you think she'll let you pick the place?"

Maggie shook her head. 'No way. She might want my input, but your Grandmother is still the headstrong woman she's been her whole life. We'll have to get her down here to make her choice and sign documents anyway. I'll give her a call when we get home and see if we can move this thing along."

Maggie had given Millie Kathleen Hannagan's address and phone number so that they might schedule a time to meet. Millie was nervous, and appreciated Maggie's offer to go with her, but in the end decided to go to the Hannagan home alone.

After speaking with Kathleen on the phone, Millie was pleased to hear that Kathleen was nervous as well. What they both wanted was to see each other as soon as possible.

Within hours, they were standing in front of each other, smiling from ear to ear.

When Kathleen came to the door, Millie knew right away that they were sisters.

"Millie?" Kathleen asked.

Millie nodded. "Yes, and you're Kathleen?

"Please, come in. Maggie told me a little about you and your situation. I must admit it was quite a shock."

"I can imagine. It was for me as well," Millie said.

"Why don't we go into the living room. I've pulled several photo albums for you to look at. There are many photos of my... our father that I'm sure you'd like to see."

They went into the living room and sat on the sofa, the photo albums stacked on the coffee table.

"I guess we should talk about the DNA test," Millie said.

"Yes, well, I have friends who have used Ancestry. I was thinking that we should start there. If the test proves that we're sisters, then I guess that's all we need to do," Kathleen suggested.

"That makes sense. Can I ask you how your family is taking this news?"

"Surprisingly well. I think they're reacting to my excitement," she said.

"So, you're happy about the possibility of us being sisters?"

Kathleen smiled. "I am. How about you?" she asked.

Millie was overjoyed to know that she hadn't upset Kathleen's family and that she was as happy about the situation as she was.

"I'm thrilled. As a matter of fact I think I'll be disappointed if it isn't true. I'm basically alone in the world. Without Maggie Moretti and her family, I'd be completely alone."

Kathleen put her hand on Millie's. "Then, let's make a plan that no matter what the results, we won't let that happen."

Millie almost cried at Kathleen's words. Through all of her research and struggles, she'd made a new friend, and that made her heart swell with gratitude. Millie felt comfort in the fact that even if they weren't bound by blood, they were already becoming family in the truest sense of the word.

After dropping Grandma Sarah off at her house, Michael and Brea headed home. They rode in silence and when they walked through the front door Brea said, "Call your mother."

She then went into Jackson's room to put him down for a nap while Quinn and Cora went downstairs to their playroom and put the tv on.

Brea went into their bedroom and shut the door.

Michael knew the signs. Brea always went into their bedroom, sat in the corner chair and stared out the window. It was her way of being alone with her thoughts, and in this case, served to parse her words to find the best way of communicating with him.

Michael went to her to try to calm the tension between them.

"Brea, we have to talk. It's not going to do any good to go off in a corner and avoid me."

"Michael, I want to know when you decided to go back to your old job? Because you never talked to me about it…not once."

He sat on the edge of the bed and looked into her eyes.

"I couldn't. I knew that whatever I said, however I explained my feelings, you wouldn't understand."

"That hurts. When has that ever happened between us? Even if I don't understand, I always listen to you and try to find a middle ground...something we can both agree on. But this? You cut me out completely."

"Brea, I can't do my job if, when I get home at the end of my shift, you're unhappy with me. It's not going to be enough just to do what I want. I need your support now more than ever."

Through tears she answered, "And I need my husband and the father of my children to come home in one piece at the end of every shift."

He closed his eyes and tried his best to let her words sink in. He moved to his knees and came close to her, taking her hand in his. "Baby, I can't imagine what you went through when I got shot. I have no doubt of the helplessness you must have felt. That's how I'd feel if anything ever happened to you and I couldn't get to you or make things better for you."

"My life would have been completely over if you'd died, Michael. I mean over...done...not wanting to go on."

He nodded as he hung his head. "I get that, but you know what? You would have gone on because no matter how you felt, you would have never let anything happen to these kids. If I was gone, you would work as a mother and a father to make sure our children lived a full and happy life because that's who you are. What I'm asking you now is to let me be who I am."

Brea pulled her hand back and looked out the window through her growing tears.

"Don't pull away. Listen to me. If I stay behind that desk one more day, I'm going to die a slow death. I won't be the man you married or the husband and father you expect from me. I'd go through the motions every day but I'd be empty inside. Do you think that the struggles I've gone through after the shooting…the hours in therapy was just about getting shot?"

She looked into his eyes. "I don't know."

"That therapy saved my life in more ways that you can imagine. The pain I felt from the bullets was nothing compared to the anguish and hopelessness I felt knowing that I was at risk of being a shell of a man. Please hear me. I need this. If you want me to be the best husband and father I can be, then you have to let me be the best police officer that I can be."

He watched his wife struggle to accept his words, but in the end that is exactly what Brea did. She wiped her eyes, placed her hands on his face, and said, "I love you, Michael Wheeler. I'm scared…but if you need this, then I support your decision."

He leaned into her and pulled her into his arms. She fell onto her knees and rested in his embrace.

CHAPTER 30

*L*auren and her grandmother called Maggie the next day with exciting news.

"We've got you on speaker, Mom. Grandma's house sold for ten thousand dollars over the asking price.

"People are crazy," Grandma said. "I figure if they want to give me more money for this place then I'll take it."

Maggie laughed at her mother's take on the whole thing.

"That's wonderful news, Mom," she said. "Sarah and I went to look at a couple of places that we think you'll love. When do you think you can get down here to check them out?"

"Closing isn't for another thirty days, and I for one would love to fly down with Grandma. I can use a little vacation. Jeff said he'll watch the girls."

"Oh, honey, that would be fantastic. I'd love to have you stay for a few days. Things are just starting to quiet down a little around here and I've got my spare bedroom, so we've got room."

"I'll book us a flight for the day after tomorrow. I've got to do a few things at the office and make sure Jeff and the girls have everything they need," Lauren said.

"Now, Maggie, don't go making a fuss just because we're visiting. It's just a few days to see the place and then we'll fly back home. Lauren will text you with our flight information."

"Sounds good. I'll let Sarah know. She'll be excited to hear that both of you are coming. Thanks for the good news."

As soon as she hung up the phone, Maggie called Sarah.

"I just talked to Lauren and Grandma. They're both coming to Captiva the day after tomorrow. Why don't you call Alissa and the other place and see if we can book another tour but this time with Grandma? I know they usually do the tours on the weekend, but Alissa said this second visit is fine any time during the week."

"That's because they figure that we're serious about buying a place. No problem. I'll give them a call. I'm so glad that Lauren is coming down as well. I miss seeing her. Did she say how she's feeling?"

"No, we didn't talk about the pregnancy, but she's in her fourth month and typically that's when you start feeling better and have more energy. I've got to run. Chelsea's coming over in a bit. She's been having a really difficult time with her sisters."

"That whole money thing with Isabelle really upset her," Sarah said.

"I know. I'm hoping I can cheer her up. I'll talk to you later."

Maggie carried her iced tea out onto the porch and thought more about Chelsea. Since moving to Captiva, Maggie had been the one with all the family troubles, drama and illness. Chelsea had been there for her every minute. She hoped that she'd be able to return the favor and help Chelsea through whatever was troubling her.

She kept her own anxieties to herself. She hadn't heard anything from the doctor about her scans and, as was the case when she was having chemotherapy and then radiation, her mind played the worst-case scenario around the clock if she didn't stay distracted. For now, she chose to believe that no news was good news.

Chelsea arrived on the back porch at exactly four o'clock in the afternoon.

"Hey stranger. How've you been?"

"I'm a liar. I told my sisters that I was having dinner over here with you and Paolo. So, what's for dinner?"

Maggie laughed. "I have no idea. I was about to eat a peach, want one?"

"Sure."

Maggie threw a peach at Chelsea who caught it as she sat in the chair next to Maggie. For a few minutes, neither of them said anything, enjoying the juicy fruit and the warm afternoon breeze.

"Where are all your guests?" Chelsea asked.

"Only one couple left. Two checked out earlier. Millie is upstairs cleaning the rooms as we speak."

"Oh, Ciara told me that Millie asked for her job back. That's wonderful. It looks like everything is working out for her."

"Yes, she's made a friend in Kathleen Hannagan. They'll know in a few days whether they're sisters or not. Either way, they're talking about getting together more often."

Chelsea grabbed a napkin to wipe the peach juice from her chin. "Don't you just love it when everything falls into place like that? I mean a month ago, would you ever have believed how things would turn out for her? I know I wouldn't have. Maybe we're all paying the price in this lifetime for things we did wrong in past lives."

Maggie searched Chelsea's face for some sign of enlightenment. "What in the world made you say that?"

Chelsea shrugged. "Oh, don't mind me. I'm just feeling upset that there is too much out of our control."

"Is that a collective and hypothetical 'our' or are you speaking about a personal experience?" Maggie asked.

"Both. I mean, think about it. In my case, I've worked so hard to have a normal and uncomplicated relationship with my sisters, and all I've experienced is drama and complications. It doesn't seem to matter what I do. They're ungrateful malcontents who won't take responsibility for anything."

Maggie had no idea what Chelsea was talking about, but as far as she could tell, Tess, Leah and Gretchen were anything but malcontents. How Maggie could sympathize with her friend without taking sides, seemed impossible. Maggie wasn't sure what to say and equally uncertain that Chelsea wanted to hear anything from her at all.

She continued to listen and say nothing.

"When we were growing up, my sisters and I fought all the time. I don't know if it was because our parents were always fighting or if it was normal sister arguments, but my memories of our childhood are of too many combative moments. Here we are all these years later and it feels like nothing has changed."

"Every family has its troubles, Chelsea. Families are made up of people, and people are complicated. Look at my family. Yes, we all love each other, but there isn't a day that goes by when there isn't something new to deal with and most of the time I feel like I'm just flying by the seat of my pants. As far as your sisters go, it's clear that they love you and want your approval."

Chelsea looked shocked at her words.

"Approval? They couldn't care less what I think. That was evident in that money grab debacle they pulled on Isabelle and Sebastian."

"Do you really believe that your sisters set out to try to get money from them? Don't you think it's possible that the whole thing evolved without any pressure from them?"

Chelsea, as stubborn as ever, shook her head. "No way. You don't know my sisters the way I do, Maggie."

Maggie didn't push the issue further. "Well, they'll be gone soon enough."

"Life around here, or at least at my house, can get back to normal. So, what's new with you?"

Maggie brought Chelsea up-to-date with everything going on with her mother.

"I can't believe she's moving down here. Talk about things getting back to normal around here. My sisters leave and your mother arrives. This should be entertaining."

"Oh, great. Now that we've solved all your family problems, you're making light of mine."

Chelsea laughed. "I'm not making light of it. It's just that your mother is quite the character and a lot of fun. Oh, I just realized the three of us can do yoga and Zumba classes in person. Won't that be fun?" Chelsea teased.

"The jury is still out on that one. We'll see."

Chelsea was still laughing in between taking bites of her peach. "Anyway, please tell me I'm getting something more than a peach for dinner."

Maggie shrugged. "To be honest, I don't know what's on the menu tonight. Let's go inside and bother Riley. The kitchen smells amazing, so I'm sure you won't be disappointed."

CHAPTER 31

*C*iara stopped by the Key Lime Garden Inn to speak with her brother and Maggie, but first searched for Millie. When she found her, Millie was sitting at the office desk refreshing her memory on how to run the bookkeeping software.

"Hey, Millie. How are you making out? Do you remember everything I taught you?"

Millie laughed. "Hardly. I'm glad you're here. Do you have a few minutes to go over some stuff with me?"

"Absolutely, but first, I need to see my brother. Give me a few minutes and I'll join you."

She went out back and found Paolo working on his car which was parked in the garage under the carriage house.

"Hey, what brings you around?" Paolo asked.

"I wanted to talk with you and Maggie about the wedding. Crawford and I have set a date and since our families are mostly here, we want to accept your offer to have the wedding on the grounds of the inn."

"That's great news. Maggie will be thrilled. We've already had three family weddings at the inn. Maybe we should advertise the inn on one of those wedding sites," he said.

"Or maybe a bridal magazine," Ciara suggested.

Maggie came up to the carriage house carrying a basket of flowers that she'd just cut from the garden. She put the basket down on top of the workbench in the garage.

"Ciara, how nice to see you. How are Crawford and the boys?"

"They're great, thanks. I already told Paolo this but Crawford and I have set a date for the wedding...June 3rd, and we'd love to have it here if you wouldn't mind. I'll do so much of the work, you'll see, you won't have to lift a finger."

"Don't be silly. I love hosting weddings at the inn. You already know what we can do, but you and I will have to get together and make it exactly as you want. I'm thrilled."

"I'm going to stop by Sarah's place on my way home. I want to ask her if she'd be my Maid of Honor."

Maggie clapped her hands together. "Sarah will be thrilled."

Ciara looked at Paolo. "And of course, I want you to give me away."

Ciara had never seen her brother cry before, but she was certain his eyes began to water.

"I'm sorry Papa isn't here for you, Ciara, but I am honored to take his place on your special day."

Ciara tried not to cry as Paolo hugged her.

Waving her hand in front of her face, she smiled. "I've got to get out of here before I start blubbering all over the place. I promised Millie that I'd sit with her and pick up where we left off. I think it's wonderful that she's back and that she's found family. You and Paolo have done a wonderful thing taking her in. Well, I'd better go."

She turned on her heels and bounced towards the inn. "Maggie, I'll talk to you later about the wedding plans, ok?"

Maggie waved. "I look forward to it."

Maggie sat on the porch swing and rocked back and forth, her eyes closed as she listened to the distant waves. The sun was almost completely gone in the sky, and another day was about to pass without her hearing from the doctor.

Even though she and Paolo didn't talk about it, Maggie instinctively knew that he was worried too.

Wiping the grease from his hands, he joined her on the porch. "I have an idea. Why don't I get in the shower and you and I go out on a date tonight?"

Maggie shook her head. "Thank you, honey, but I'm not really in the mood. I'm sort of tired. Maybe another night?"

Paolo nodded. "Of course. I need that shower anyway. I'll come down and join you after I'm clean."

"I'm going to take a walk. I'll probably be back by the time you come down," she said.

He kissed her forehead and went across to the carriage house.

It was in moments like these, when she sat alone on her swing or on the bench near the koi pond, or even among the hedges, bushes and trellis of the garden, that Maggie found her peace. The Key Lime Garden Inn had become something of a hidden and magical place for her as it had for Rose Johnson Lane when she was alive.

Hearing the tree frogs amongst the sounds of the windchimes, waves, and music from town, Maggie felt more in her element than anywhere else in the world.

Each year while living in Massachusetts, she'd worked for hours in her garden trying to create an oasis where she could hide from the difficulties and stresses in her life. Whenever life got to be too much to handle, she'd sneak out to her garden and find little moments of peace.

Daniel used to tell everyone that his wife would hide away when she went to the garden. He was making fun of her, but he was right about her hiding. She'd imagine herself tiny as she walked along the stone paths and walkways that she'd created to meander through their one-acre property.

She'd done the same within the Key Lime Garden Inn gardens only on a much larger scale. She and Paolo had incorporated fountains and sculptures, a gazebo and whimsical elements as well as two hammocks and a wooden bench near the pond. Raised flower beds separated the herb and vegetable gardens that peppered the landscape which provided most of the kitchen's farm-to-table cuisine.

However, the hideaway that she'd created on Captiva Island was her celebration of life in all its glory, while her hideaway in Massachusetts was quite simply designed to save her life.

What Daniel didn't understand was that Maggie didn't just hide away in her garden, she had hidden away in every corner of her home. From her sewing room to the greenhouse, she had created small coffins for herself instead of letting the light in where she'd be forced to look at what was wrong in her marriage.

Now her life was filled with sunlight and joy almost every day and she no longer felt the need to hide away. Her garden was still the place where she could enjoy solitude and prayer, but it would never become a place for her to hide from the rest of the world.

She walked through the walkway to the beach and looked at the full moon lighting up everything around her. She could hear Paolo calling from the porch, his voice louder as he approached.

"Maggie! Didn't you hear me calling you?" he asked.

"I'm sorry, I guess I was deep in thought. Look at this moon. Isn't it incredible?"

"There was a message on the landline. The doctor's office called and left a message for you to call them back. He called a couple of hours ago."

Maggie had gone from pure bliss to terror in the blink of an eye. "Why didn't he call my cellphone?" she asked.

"The message said he tried but it kept ringing and then went nowhere. I have no idea. You've got to call the doctor. They said even if it's after hours, call his cell."

"Oh, this stupid phone. Sarah set up all these darn ringtones and now I have no idea how to answer my phone when a call comes that doesn't have a ringtone."

Maggie held on to Paolo's arm as her thumb hit the doctor's cellphone number.

"Hello, Maggie,"

"Dr. Renolt, hello. I'm so sorry that I missed your call earlier."

"No problem at all. I didn't want you to have to wait for the results. They came in this morning. No evidence of cancer anywhere."

Maggie's hand let go of Paolo's arm and reached for her throat. She looked at Paolo. "Are you sure?"

Dr. Renolt laughed. "Yes, Maggie, I'm sure. You do not have any cancer in your body. Now go out and celebrate with your husband. We'll see you in six months."

"Thank you, Doctor. Thank you so much," she said.

Maggie ended the call and turned to Paolo. "No cancer."

She threw her body into Paolo's with such force, they fell onto the sand and laughed.

"Say it again," he said.

"No cancer in my body. That's what he said."

They held each other for a while and then laid on their backs to look at the stars. Maggie smiled and realized that she'd never felt more alive than she did right now.

CHAPTER 32

*S*ince the night of Isabelle's party, Chelsea and her sisters avoided talking about Key West and The CoiffeeShop. Tess, Leah and Gretchen kept to themselves most of the time, and one afternoon Chelsea overheard them talking about leaving Captiva days earlier than they'd planned.

As angry and frustrated as Chelsea was with her sisters' behavior, she had moments of deep regret for their inability to mend fences and find a way to be closer, and she had to admit that she was as much to blame for that as they were.

Memories from her childhood were hard to push aside in the interest of family unity, but there was much to love about her sisters and their accomplishments.

Tess, with her long, wavy hair and independent spirit; Leah, gentle and petite, with her love of animals and determination; and Gretchen, strong and assertive, who had overcome hardship in the form of abuse from an alcoholic husband. All three deserved respect for how they'd never given up in the face of adversity and personal struggle.

However throughout their childhood, their parents' frequent fights and conflicts forced the sisters into a perpetual state of being pitted against one another. Chelsea hated how their parents used their children as a way to get back at each other. Their parents' divorce was inevitable, and the sisters' separation unavoidable.

In the early morning hours, Chelsea's sisters were in the kitchen filling their coffee mugs when she joined them.

"Do you think it's possible for the four of us to hang out today instead of it just being the three of us?" Tess asked Chelsea.

Chelsea's back was to her sisters as she poured coffee into her mug. "I'm not sure. I've got a few errands I have to do. Maybe later."

"Why are you avoiding us?" Gretchen asked.

Chelsea turned to face them. "I'm not trying to avoid you."

"Yes, you are," Leah asserted. "I don't know why we even came to Captiva. You haven't wanted us here from the start."

"You don't know why you came to Captiva?" Chelsea replied. "I'll tell you why you wanted to come here, to get money for your Key West adventure. Well, I guess you got what you came for... congratulations."

"That's it!" Gretchen protested. "I've had it. You continue to stay in this righteous place of superiority when there is nothing superior about you. You live on an island Paradise where everything is perfect and you can pretend that you've always lived a life of privilege. Our childhood can't touch you here, but there is something you haven't considered. It doesn't matter how insulated and protected you make your environment, you still have to live with yourself and your past. You hated Dad and you've hated us because we went to live with him...because we took his side in that terrible marriage."

Chelsea couldn't believe that Gretchen was attacking her this way.

"We didn't really have a choice now, did we?" Chelsea asked.

Gretchen laughed at Chelsea's words, "No choice? You had a choice of whether to go with Dad or Mom and you chose Mom, who cheated on Dad more than once. She wasn't the mother you pretend she was, and you know it."

"Gretchen, stop!" Leah begged. "We can't change the past. Let it go."

Tess's voice, soft and low, added her perspective. "Gretchen, why don't you tell Chelsea why you're really upset?"

"What?" Gretchen asked.

"You're not upset that she chose Mom, you're upset that she didn't choose us."

Tess looked at Chelsea. "We all were upset about that. Hours of therapy helped me see the reason I was so rebellious growing up." She looked at Leah. "And what about you? How many times did you tell me that you lacked confidence to make your way in the world?"

Gretchen directed her next words to Chelsea. "I don't mind telling you that I've spent many hours in therapy myself. No one is blaming you for all of it, but you can't keep acting as if none of it has touched and traumatized you as well. You act as if what we all went through never affected you, but I see how you live your life now. Still hiding behind Mom's skirt."

"What are you talking about?" Chelsea demanded.

"I've seen your paintings. I know about your showing at the gallery. I've looked at several of your creations."

She looked at Tess and Leah. "Do you know how our sister signs her art? Every painting is signed with the initials CL… Chelsea Lawrence. Not her married name, Chelsea Marsden. That's because she still identifies as that little girl who loved a mother who didn't care one bit about her."

Chelsea was seething. "How dare you come into my home and talk to me like this? What I do with my art is my business and not only has nothing to do with you, but it is also my prerogative to be as creative as I want…my name is mine to do with as I wish."

"Please, both of you, stop now before you say things you can't take back," Leah pleaded.

Chelsea looked directly into Gretchen's eyes. "I'd say that time has come and gone. You all are welcome to move on to Key West any time you wish. I won't stay in this room and listen to your accusations one more minute."

Chelsea grabbed her purse, walked out of the house and got into her car. She had no idea where she was going, but she knew that she needed to drive as far as she could to get away from the house and her sisters.

Without a plan, her instinct was to stay away as long as she could and, if necessary, stay in a hotel so that when she returned home, her sisters would be gone.

Leaning on her cane, Grandma walked ahead of Lauren as they walked out of the gate and toward Maggie.

Lauren carried both her carry-on and her grandmother's.

Waving, she called her mother. "Mom!"

Maggie hugged Lauren and then her mother. She knew she'd get blowback for asking, but she did it anyway.

"Mom, should we get a wheelchair?"

Based on her mother's reaction, Maggie decided that if looks could kill, she'd be dead on the floor at Gate D3 in the Southwest Florida International Airport.

"I don't know, do you need one?" her mother asked sarcastically.

Maggie sighed. "Ok, then. Let's go. How was your flight?"

"This is the second time JetBlue gave us a bag of M&Ms for breakfast. What is that about?" Grandma asked.

"I don't know, Mom. Maybe they want your blood sugar raised at six in the morning."

"That didn't stop me from eating my bag and Grandma's," Lauren added. She rubbed her stomach and smiled. "I'm blaming it on this little one."

"Careful about that," Maggie warned. "You might be contributing to the baby's early sugar addiction."

They got to the car and Lauren placed the luggage in the trunk.

"I figured we would go straight to Marina Bluff Estates. Sarah said she'd meet us there. Then, we'll hop over to Sunset Harbor Springs. Riley and Iris are making us a nice lunch too. We'll probably be starving when we're done."

"I'm hungry now," her mother announced. "What do you expect when you think you're going to get a nice breakfast on the plane?"

Maggie worried that her mother might not be able to tour both places while her ankle was hurting. That, plus not eating breakfast was a concern.

"Do you want to stop and get something to eat before we get there? We can go to Starbucks and get a muffin or something."

Her mother waved her off and looked out the window. "No. I'll do the best I can."

Maggie looked in the rearview at Lauren who was trying not to laugh.

Alissa Mayer and Sarah met them in the parking lot with a six-passenger golf cart. "I thought you all might appreciate the ride, especially with your mother's ankle injury."

Maggie's mother smiled and nodded. "Thank you so much. How thoughtful of you. It's nice to know that some people think ahead."

Maggie looked at Lauren and rolled her eyes. It had begun. Her mother's perpetual irritation directed only at her family, while appearing pleasant to everyone else. Alissa must have thought her mother a perfect angel.

Grandma Sarah got in the front with Alissa and Maggie, Sarah and Lauren got in the back rows.

"We'll do an expansive drive around so that you can see just how much we have here. Then, I'll take you to the two homes that are available now. From what your family has told me, you're quite an independent woman."

"I certainly am, and I'm glad to hear that they know it," Grandma Sarah replied.

"Well, Marina Bluff Estates prides itself on supporting people, especially women, like yourself."

It was hard to know whether Marina Bluff Estates, Alissa Mayer or the prospect of a future without snow had softened her mother in the last fifteen minutes, but Maggie was grateful for the change, albeit brief.

Except for the square footage, the two homes were laid out completely different from one another. Maggie could tell which of the two her mother would pick because she loved the first one which was the farthest away from all activity, and her mother hated to be so far away from people.

Based on the proximity to the main building, the clubhouse, pool and theater, her mother would want to be where the action was.

"I like the second one," her mother announced.

Maggie smiled at her accuracy and was glad to know that she still had talent for knowing her mother so well.

Sarah and Lauren nodded. "That's our favorite too," Lauren said. "You won't have to go too far to have fun."

"Exactly," her mother answered and then turned to Maggie. "You see how my grandchildren know me so well? That's because Lauren has been hanging with me so much, and Sarah is my namesake."

Maggie nodded and smiled at her daughters. "They're pretty smart," Maggie said.

"Of course they are. They take after me."

When the tour was over, her mother didn't want to go to Sunset Harbor Springs. "I want to live here. I'll take the second house," she announced.

"Are you sure, Grandma?" Sarah asked.

"I'm sure. When can I move in?"

"Technically, you can move in fairly soon. We can get the closing done quickly. We don't offer contingency clauses and I know you are trying to sell your property in Massachusetts."

Grandma Sarah turned to look at Lauren.

"What does that mean?" she asked.

"It's not an issue Grandma. It means they won't sell the house to you if you need to sell your home up north first. Your house is already sold. Do you need the funds from the sale to buy this one?"

"Of course I do. I'm not made of money, you know."

Everyone smiled. Lauren explained to Alissa. "The buyers wanted to close quickly. I'm the one who expected it would take longer to find something down here. We can move the closing up and my grandmother is already prepared to sign the P&S today if we can."

"Perfect. Let's go back to my office and fill out all the paperwork," Alissa said.

"I'll get in touch with the other real estate agent and explain. Her buyers will be pleased."

"How long is this paperwork signing going to take? I haven't eaten anything all morning."

Alissa smiled. "How about I have one of our chefs bring you something to eat? He will make you anything that you'd like."

Grandma Sarah's face lit up. "That would be wonderful."

She turned and looked at Maggie, pleased that someone was already jumping into action the minute she asked for something.

Maggie didn't bother to remind her mother that a delicious lunch awaited them upon their return to the Key Lime Garden Inn. She figured there would be no point since her mother would most likely eat that meal as well.

CHAPTER 33

*H*ours had passed and it was almost dark before Chelsea returned to Captiva Island. She'd driven as far away as Tampa before she turned around and headed home.

It wasn't her nature to cry. The last time she did was when her husband died. However, all afternoon, as she drove north, she had to stop several times when she couldn't see because her eyes were filled with tears.

By the time she traveled over the Sanibel Bridge, she blew the air conditioner fan on her face to hide her red eyes.

As she approached her house, she saw that her sisters' car rental was gone, and once inside the house the truth was clear. They'd left a note on the glass table in the foyer, but Chelsea wouldn't open it. She waited an hour before pouring herself a glass of wine and carried it to the lanai. She took a deep breath and opened the letter.

Dear Chelsea,

. . .

After so many years, all three of us had hoped for a better outcome on this trip. It's impossible to take back what was said today, just as it's impossible to change the past.

There are so many things that we'd like to say to you, but we can't do it in this letter and right now we feel it's better to leave and let some time and distance help us to find our way back to each other eventually.

After you left, we talked and each of us admitted that more than anything we want you to think well of us. We're not sure what it's going to take to accomplish that, but we hope you'll take some time to think about who we are and see us in a different light.

If that is too difficult, then perhaps it's because you don't know us well. We can't blame you completely for that, but, going forward, if you'd like to get to know us as grown women and sisters who love you, maybe you'll find your way to Key West one of these days.

Mom and Dad wasted so many years in anger. Let's not do the same.

Love,

Tess, Leah and Gretchen

Chelsea's face rested in her hand as the letter fell onto her lap, and she cried once more.

Maggie's mother finished her dinner and announced that she was going to bed. The travel from Boston followed by the visit to Marina Bluff Estates exhausted her. Lauren went to Sarah and Trevor's for the night, and Paolo went upstairs to the carriage house to watch baseball.

She decided to walk to Chelsea's house to say goodbye to Tess, Leah and Gretchen. Although Chelsea and her sisters struggled to see eye-to-eye on this trip, she hoped that things were beginning to settle down between them.

She grabbed her wallet and keys and walked to Chelsea's house.

Chelsea's car was in the driveway, but her sisters' car rental was not. The lights were off inside the house but she decided to knock on the front door anyway. Peering inside the glass, she couldn't see anyone in the living room, so she decided to walk around to the back of the house in the hopes that she'd be able to enter through the lanai screen door.

When she reached the lanai, she could see Chelsea sitting in the dark on the outdoor loveseat.

"Chelsea?"

Her friend didn't answer.

"Honey? What's wrong?"

Chelsea handed Maggie her sisters' note. When Maggie finished reading it, she looked at Chelsea.

"What happened? Why did they leave early? What did you all say to each other?"

Chelsea took a sip of her wine and shrugged. "What didn't we say? We've been holding on to so much for so long, it was like the floodgates opened and everything came spilling out."

"Surely you all can fix this in time," Maggie said.

Chelsea shook her head. "I don't think so, Mags. We've tried this before and it never ends well. Do you remember me referencing their visit as an impending doomsday? I was right. Look what happened. I should never have allowed them to come here."

Maggie sat next to Chelsea and shook her head. "I don't think even you have the right to tell someone they can't come to Captiva. They wanted to see you, you guys tried to get along and it didn't work out. That doesn't mean you give up."

"Really, Tinkerbell? Why not? Why do I have to keep doing this over and over again?"

"Don't get sarcastic with me. Maybe you need some perspective here. Millie Brenner has no one. She's done everything in her power to find family, and here you are throwing it all away like it means nothing. I love you, Chelsea, but honestly, this whole trip while your sisters were here you've been a real jerk."

Shocked at Maggie's assessment of her behavior, Chelsea didn't know how to respond. It was bad enough that Chelsea had fought with her sisters but something else entirely to now be fighting with her best friend.

Maggie reached for her wallet and opened it, pulling out a small, folded envelope. "Here, this is for you," she said.

Maggie shrugged. "I don't know. Gretchen gave it to me a few days ago and made me promise that I wouldn't give it to you until after they'd left. I came over here tonight to say goodbye to them because I knew they were leaving tomorrow. I had no idea they'd be gone, but since they are, I guess I can give this to you now."

Chelsea opened the envelope and found Sebastian's check for twenty-five thousand dollars, ripped in half.

She looked at Maggie and held up the check.

"They didn't cash Sebastian's check after all. Why didn't they tell me they weren't going to keep the money? They made me think the worst."

Maggie shook her head. "No they didn't, Chelsea. You did that all on your own."

Chelsea leaned back and sighed. "You're absolutely right," Chelsea said.

"About?"

"I've been a complete jerk," Chelsea answered.

Maggie nodded. "Yup. But I love you anyway."

Chelsea half-smiled at her friend's sentiment.

'Oh Maggie, I'm so sorry. I've been so absorbed with my own problems I never thought to ask you about your test results. Have they come back yet?"

Maggie smiled and nodded. "No evidence of cancer."

Chelsea screamed and hugged Maggie tight. "This is the best news I've had all day. I'm so happy I could burst."

Maggie shook her head and laughed. "Isn't life funny? One minute you feel so bad you can hardly breathe, and the next you're practically euphoric."

"I don't know about funny, but life certainly is strange, and I don't mind telling you that I'm getting too old for this roller-coaster."

Not since Christmas had Lauren seen Sarah and Trevor's children, and she didn't want to return to Massachusetts without spending time with them.

"Sarah, you and Trevor have made your home so beautiful. If I were you, I'd never want to leave," Lauren said.

"It hasn't been easy with three kids under seven years old. When we built the addition, it inspired me to rework the entire house decor. I figured the addition couldn't have one vibe and the rest of the house something different. I can't take credit for the outcome though. Don't tell anyone but we hired an interior designer for the project. I wanted clean, uncluttered, minimalistic designs in greens, blues, turquoise and tan with lots of rattan and an open concept."

"It's such a different look from the way we grew up. I mean with everything open like this, I'd be running around freaking out if a fly came inside," Lauren remarked.

"It's funny you should say that because when I first moved here, that's one of the things I was worried about. Trevor kept telling me to trust him, and that bugs would not be an issue, and he was right. If something comes flying in here, it only continues on its journey by flying out the other side of the house. The plus side is getting this incredible view of the ocean. You feel like you're living right on the beach."

"How do you keep it so clean, though? This uncluttered look is wonderful but with three kids I don't know how you do it."

Sarah laughed. "I have someone come in once a week to straighten up the place, clean the bathroom, dust, vacuum...all the things I hate to do. This way, I get to spend more time with the kids. Although now that I'm not working outside the house, that little luxury might have to go away. We'll see if I can do it myself before I let my housecleaner go."

"How is that going...being home with the kids, I mean?"

"It's not even been a week. Ask me in a few months. How about you? How are you managing the balance of work and home life?"

Lauren shrugged. "I can't take one bit of credit for it. I'd hate to have you think that I'm supermom with one hand baking cookies while I'm closing a real estate deal on the phone at the same time. It's nothing like that. With Jeff being a stay-at-home dad, my work is easier and my time with the girls is less stressful. When I went back to work, I worried about the kids, and then when I was at home, I'd worry about work. Now that Jeff has taken over running the house and taking care of the girls, I get to enjoy whatever I'm doing when I'm doing it and don't have to worry.``

"I'm glad things worked out for you and Jeff. I could never see Trevor staying at home with the kids full-time. He didn't like working with his father at first. As a matter of fact, I did worry about what he'd do for a career. He was such a laidback, worldly guy who traveled the globe working non-profits and volunteering. I thought to myself at the time that I'd be the one to bring in the money. But, once he went to work with his father...well, money hasn't been a problem since. I assume things are going to change once you have the baby?"

Lauren nodded. "I'll be home for several months but since I own the real estate firm, I can work it out however I need to. I'm assuming that I'll go into the office here and there and will bring the baby with me."

"Sounds good," Sarah said. "I've got a bigger question for you. How do you think Mom and Grandma are going to get along once Grandma moves down here? I'm a bit nervous about it."

Lauren laughed. "Good question. Honestly, I've seen

Grandma changing somewhat in the last few months. I think she's struggling with wanting to keep her independence and realizing that she might need help in the coming years. It's a rough time for her, but I see her softening a bit."

"I guess we'll find out soon enough," Sarah said.

"I'm passing the baton to you and Mom. I've been dealing with Grandma ever since Mom and you moved down here. You're going to have to find her a new doctor and dentist and heaven knows what else. The good thing is now you have a smaller, select group to choose from. Everything she's going to need is right at Marina Bluff Estates."

"I'll keep you updated on our progress. Wish me luck."

"You'll need more than luck, Sarah. You're going to need all the patience you can muster," Lauren answered.

CHAPTER 34

On her early morning walk, Maggie couldn't shake the feeling that she was being followed. It was only six-thirty, she was still somewhat sleepy and ignored the feeling. But, after walking half a mile, she turned and noticed a dog slowly keeping pace with her.

She stopped and waited for it to catch up to her, assuming there would be a human following behind. Maggie looked around and waited but saw no one. The dog seemed friendly enough and so she sat on the sand and watched to see what it would do next.

Maggie couldn't tell what breed of dog it was, but her heart melted the minute it sat next to her, leaning its body against hers.

The dog didn't have a name tag, a collar or anything to help find its owner, and Maggie wondered how a dog could find its way to this part of the beach.

It must live in one of these houses and somehow get out.

The only solution was to walk up and down the beach until someone came out of the house and called the dog. Maggie called Paolo and let him know what she was doing, and to contact anyone he knew along Andy Rosse and the other connecting streets.

She didn't worry that they'd find the dog's owner. It was just a matter of time. Perhaps the dog jumped out of a car. There had been so many tourists in the area, Maggie thought that would be the next place she'd look if none of the homeowners near the beach claimed the dog.

"How did you get here, you little cutie?" she asked the pup.

No matter which direction Maggie took, the dog stayed close to her and wouldn't budge. If she stopped, the dog stopped. If she sat on the sand, the dog would do the same. It was the strangest thing she'd ever seen, for a dog to be so friendly.

Paolo called her back. "Is the dog still with you?"

"Yes. This dog is sticking to me like glue."

"She's a girl and her name is Lulu. She's old man Crandall's dog. I guess she got out of his yard and made it out onto the beach."

"That's great news that you found her family. I'll walk the dog up to his house and then I'll be in to have breakfast."

"Ok, hon. See you soon."

Maggie looked at the dog and rubbed her head. "Looks like we found your owner. He must be worried sick. Come on, let's get you back home."

The dog continued to obey Maggie's words. As they walked down the beach toward Jared Crandall's home, Maggie had a twinge of sadness at not being able to keep the dog. She had no idea what made her think this way. She'd never wanted a pet while living on Captiva. She liked her freedom to come and go as she pleased. But Lulu was so cute, Maggie immediately fell in love.

Jared Crandall was out on his porch when Maggie and Lulu reached his home. Once they walked up the pathway to the house, Lulu ran to her owner.

"I always take her on the beach for walks every day, but this time, she went without me."

Maggie laughed. "How are you doing Mr. Crandall?"

"Oh, you know. I'm getting old. Got lots of the usual aches and pains."

"You and me, both," Maggie said. "It's good that you walk on the beach though. That's one of the best exercises, for you and for Lulu."

"Yes, that's what my wife keeps telling me," he answered.

"Does your wife walk with you and Lulu?"

"Oh, yes. The three of us get along just fine. Thank you for asking. Well, thanks for bringing Lulu home. My wife was just about to get in the car and drive around Captiva looking for her. I'm not sure what I would have done without this old girl. She's family, you know."

Maggie smiled. "I understand. These sweet pets really are members of the family. Anyway, I'll get back home. I'm glad I was able to help. Say hello to Mrs. Crandall please."

"Will do." He waved, and Lulu watched as Maggie walked away.

———

When she got to the inn, Maggie found Paolo on the back porch drinking his coffee.

"How'd it go?" he asked.

"Lulu is back where she belongs," Maggie answered. "Let me get a cup of coffee and I'll join you."

She poured herself a cup and went back outside to the porch swing.

"It's another beautiful Florida morning. Not a cloud in the sky," Paolo said.

Maggie nodded. "Don't laugh at me, but what would you say if I said I wanted to get a dog?"

Paolo looked at her. "I'm not laughing."

"Don't make jokes. I'm serious. You should have seen Lulu. She was practically glued to me."

"So, you can visit Lulu anytime you want. She lives just a stone's throw from here."

"It's not the same. I really think I want to go look for a puppy."

"A puppy? That's a whole different animal. Puppies need so much attention. Aren't we crazy busy here already? Do you really think that we have the time and patience for a puppy?" he asked.

"I do. Plus, it would be great for the grandkids. I think they'd have so much fun when they come to visit."

"Well, if you're really serious about it we can drive up to the shelter in Fort Myers. I'm not sure about a puppy though. Does the dog have to be a puppy?"

Maggie hadn't thought about it before, but since Paolo asked, she realized that the right dog was more important than the dog being a puppy. "No, I guess it doesn't," she answered.

"When do you want to do this?"

"I don't know, at least not until my mother and Lauren go back to Boston. I've got enough on my plate dealing with her situation."

"Ok. After your mother leaves, we'll go see what they have at the shelter," he said. "Do you care what breed it is?"

Maggie shook her head. "Not at all. I'm a believer that the right dog will pick us."

Paolo nodded. "That's how it usually works."

Grandma Sarah came downstairs calling for Maggie.

"We're out here on the back porch, Mom," Maggie yelled.

She joined them on the porch and immediately started complaining. "Did you know that when your father and I used to stay in a hotel, I would make the bed before we went out for the day?"

Maggie smiled. "No, Mom. I didn't know that."

"I'm telling you for a reason. I just walked by the room that your guests are staying in, you know, the ones that are in the dining room eating breakfast?"

"And?"

"And we were all coming down at the same time, so I saw that they hadn't made their bed."

"Mom, it's no one's business what my guests are doing, but most of the time, the rest of us like to go on vacation and get away from everyday chores. That's one of the perks of being on vacation."

"Maybe so, but I set them straight," she said.

Maggie jumped up off the porch swing. "You what?"

"I told them what I just told you, that your father and I always left our room neat before we left for the day."

Maggie looked at Paolo for help. Distraught over her mother's interference, she headed inside and to the dining room.

When she got there she only saw the husband. "Good morning. Is your wife joining you?"

Like a gentleman, he stood when Maggie approached. "No, please sit down," she said.

"Yes, she just went back upstairs for a moment," he said.

Maggie had an idea why.

"I hope my other guest didn't upset the two of you earlier. That's my mother. She is going back home later today, and well... please tell me that your wife didn't go back upstairs to make the bed."

He laughed. "No. She forgot her purse."

Relieved to hear it, she said, "Thank goodness. Please, enjoy your breakfast, and don't worry about the bed or anything else."

Trying to make Maggie feel better, he said, "If it helps any, I've got a grandmother just like her. She adds a bit of color to our family."

Maggie smiled. "She adds color, all right. Thank you for saying that. Enjoy your day."

Maggie returned to the porch but her mother wasn't there. "Where's my mother?"

"She went upstairs to make sure that Lauren made her bed before going over to Sarah's yesterday."

Maggie shook her head. "We can do this, right?"

"What, the puppy?"

"No. My mother. I think the puppy will be a breeze by comparison."

Paolo laughed. "Don't worry. Together we can handle anything...even your mother."

———————

Chelsea stopped over for her morning coffee and cranberry-walnut scones.

"What's a morning at the Key Lime Garden Inn without me here?" she asked.

"Paolo and I were just asking ourselves that very question. Good morning, Chelsea."

"We'll see," Chelsea answered as she scurried into the kitchen to get a cup.

Paolo kissed Maggie and got up from the swing. "Well, I'm off to Sanibellia. I'll be back later to say goodbye to your mother and Lauren. Is she back from Sarah's yet?"

"Not yet. She should be along soon though. Their flight is at six tonight so they've got plenty of time," Maggie answered.

Chelsea came out to the porch and placed her dish on the table. "I hope I didn't run off Paolo."

"You didn't. He had to get to work. So, let me tell you about my morning. It's eight-thirty but it feels more like two in the afternoon."

Maggie explained about the dog and about her mother's comment to her guests.

Chelsea laughed. "My goodness, you have had a morning. Where's your mother now?"

Just then, Grandma Sarah came out to join them. "Here I am. Good morning, Chelsea. It's nice to see you."

"Good morning. It's nice to see you again too. I hear that you're going back home today."

"Yes, I've still got so much to do before the move. What about you Chelsea? I haven't heard a thing about what's been going on with you."

Maggie could see that her mother was putting Chelsea on the spot and that her friend didn't want to be rude.

Trying to change the subject, Maggie asked, "Mom, how is your ankle? I see that you're not using your cane this morning."

Still eyeing Chelsea, her mother said, "It feels better. I could probably do with a walk. The doctor said I should move."

"That sounds great. Let me just finish my coffee and…"

"No. Not you. Chelsea," she said.

"What?" Maggie asked.

"Chelsea, why don't you and I go for a walk around the garden?"

Chelsea put her coffee down on the table and got up. "If you'd like," she answered.

Maggie watched the two of them go down the stairs and around through the garden. Chelsea turned once, looked at her, and shrugged.

Whatever her mother was up to, Maggie hadn't the slightest idea, but she wasn't worried. Chelsea could hold her own, even against Sarah Garrison.

"How old are you, Chelsea? If you don't mind my asking?"

Taken aback, Chelsea answered, "I'm fifty-six. Why?"

"Fifty-six. I remember those days like it was yesterday. I was just starting to go through 'the change.' My body was so confused and so was I. I felt like it was betraying me. It had cooperated for so long, I took for granted that it would always do what I wanted it to. Can you imagine how silly I was?"

Chelsea had no idea where Maggie's mother was going with this information, so all she could do was smile, nod, and agree with everything she said. It wasn't Chelsea's style to do so, but she figured what would it hurt since Grandma Sarah was leaving the island in a few hours.

They came upon the wooden bench near the koi pond. "Shall we sit?" Chelsea asked.

"Good idea."

They sat in silence admiring the fish and listening to the windchimes that Paolo had put near the bench. The bird bath was filled with birds cleaning themselves, and an occasional blue jay disrupted them, sending the smaller birds flying to the nearest tree.

"So, Chelsea, what is it that you're holding on to?" Grandma Sarah asked.

"I'm sorry?" Chelsea answered.

"You must be holding on to something to be so unhappy."

Chelsea chuckled. "I'm not unhappy."

"Sure you are. It takes time to understand what's going on, but I'm going to save you time and money."

"Time and money?" Chelsea asked.

"Absolutely. Those therapists charge a lot and you have to go for months and months...sometimes even years. I'm going to save you all that."

Chelsea tried not to laugh and sat quietly waiting for the inevitable words of wisdom that only Maggie's mother could impart.

"Look at me, for instance. You should see all the junk I've been holding on to up in my attic, down in the basement, over in the garage and shed. When we had the yard sale we threw out so much stuff, I couldn't believe it."

"Didn't you try to sell the stuff?"

"Oh, sure. I did sell a lot. I made a killing. In the end it was almost eight hundred dollars."

"Wow, that's great."

Chelsea still wasn't sure what the woman was trying to say.

"Anyway, even with the money I made, I was acutely aware that I'd kept so many things from my past. I still have Maggie's baptism outfit for heaven's sake. Not my *grandchildren's* stuff, but my children's things. My son and other daughter couldn't care less about coming to visit me, and here I was holding on to things from when they were children."

"Well, to be fair, isn't that what most of us do?" Chelsea asked.

"Exactly my point. We all do it, and do you know why?"

"I assume because it brings back fond memories. Isn't that why you kept everything from when your children were little?"

"Chelsea, we all hold on to things that we shouldn't. Why? Because we've given those things power. It doesn't matter whether it's an object, or a feeling. It can be anger, resentment, hurt, money, a memory or a piece of jewelry. The only way to break free and take that power back is to see the thing for what it is…the thing that keeps us from moving on. I've held on to my children's things because I wasn't able to live in the present with clarity. I didn't want to move forward because forward might mean pain, and I wanted to avoid that more than anything. So, I'll ask you again. What are you holding on to?"

Chelsea thought about what Grandma Sarah was saying and her first thought was of her sisters and the belief that somehow she had never shown her sisters the love they deserved. She'd assumed that they hated her for taking their mother's side, but they didn't hate her at all. They wanted her to love them and she needed them to be in her life. These were things she had held on to most of her life and it kept her family separated for much of it.

Grandma Sarah got up from the bench.

"Once you figure it out, you'll let it go…all of it, just like I have."

Grandma Sarah started for the back porch and stopped just long enough to pull some weeds from a few plants.

"When I move down here, I'm going to have to show Paolo how to do a better job in this garden."

Chelsea watched her as the woman headed for the inn and felt joy knowing soon Maggie's mother would be part of her world just as she had been for her family for many years.

CHAPTER 35

It was three days after Lauren and Grandma Sarah
returned to Massachusetts. Chelsea had finally made
good on her promise to drag Maggie to Zumba class.

"You're going to love it," Chelsea said.

"Did I mention that I researched it last night and saw some of
the steps? I'm not sure I'll be very good at this."

"Oh, come on. I was a beginner once, and might I remind you
that your mother is doing it," Chelsea teased.

"Was…she was doing it until she sprained her ankle. Who
knows what I'll sprain today," Maggie answered.

The class was filled with only women. Six women Maggie had
never met before came up to her. "Welcome, Maggie. Chelsea
told us that you'd be joining us today."

Maggie smiled and figured she'd make the best of it if she
wanted to outpace her mother in Zumba class.

"I'm happy to be here," Maggie lied.

"I'm Ellen and I'll let everyone else introduce themselves to
you. I run the class, and all you have to do is follow me as best
you can. Don't worry about being perfect. This is your first time

and all of us have, at one time or another, been where you are today. You'll get the hang of it in time."

Ellen moved to the front of the class and one-by-one the other woman shook her hand and then quickly got in place behind Ellen.

How hard can this be? It's a bit like following the leader. I can do that.

The music started and it was a Ricky Martin song, and one she had never heard before. Everyone swayed to the beat in effortless motions. It seemed to Maggie that every single body part was used. Her arms lifted, stretched, and swirled and her legs moved from side to side and back and forth.

The music continued from one song to the next and the women continued to dance without stopping. Everyone followed Ellen, who seemed relaxed, as if each motion was fluid and graceful.

Maggie, on the other hand, could see her face redden in the mirror across the room. At first nothing about Zumba felt difficult, but over several minutes, it was clear to her that she was more out of shape than she realized.

Chelsea wasn't out of breath at all. She fit in with everyone else but Maggie's face and body was hot, red and wet. She felt like a lobster just coming out of a boiling pot of water, and it didn't feel good.

She looked over at Chelsea and waved. "I think I need to sit….here, on the floor…now."

To her credit, Chelsea stopped dancing and tended to her best friend. A gesture Maggie appreciated considering the look Ellen gave her.

"She'll be all right, Chelsea. You can keep dancing. Maggie, you join back in just as soon as you're able," Ellen said.

"Is she out of her mind?" Maggie whispered. "I don't expect I'll be able to anytime soon. If you want to keep dancing, I'll meet you next door at Starbucks. I'll be the one in the corner booth with paramedics checking my heart rate."

Maggie's situation must have struck Chelsea as funny because she began to giggle as she tried to lift Maggie off the floor. Maggie laughed out loud and soon, the two of them were laughing so hard, Chelsea had to apologize to the group as they walked out of the Zumba class and into the Starbucks next door.

"Do you think they'll kick you out of the Zumba club...I mean, class?" Maggie asked.

"I think they'll let me back in...you, not so much."

They got their coffee and sat in the corner booth...no paramedics needed.

"Hey, did I mention that we need to have an emergency lunch-bunch meeting?"

"Are our friends trying to copy my Code Red alarm system?" Maggie asked.

"No, nothing like that. Jane is getting married," Chelsea announced.

"What? I never would have believed it. She said she'd never get married...ever. How did this happen? Is she still with that guy from the law firm?"

Chelsea shook her head. "No. He's a dentist."

"A dentist? I never would have imagined that Jane would marry a dentist," Maggie said.

"Why not? What's wrong with a dentist?"

"Nothing, it's just that Jane's life is rather glamorous. She's always traveling and the guys that she goes out with take her to the most exotic places. Can you picture a dentist doing that?"

Chelsea smiled. "Maybe not, but it doesn't matter. She's in love and that's all there is to that."

Maggie sipped her coffee, "So, why the emergency meeting?"

"Brace yourself. She wants the girls to come back down to Captiva for her bachelorette party."

Maggie almost spit out her coffee. "Are you serious? The last time we tried that, Rachel went into labor on a boat in the middle of my party."

Chelsea laughed. "I remember. That was so much fun."

"When do they want to have the meeting?"

"This afternoon," Chelsea responded, knowing Maggie would flip.

Maggie's eyes went wide. "Nothing like a last-minute notice."

"She called me yesterday but with everything going on, I just forgot about it. Still, you're right, not much notice."

"I guess we ought to get going then. I need a shower before I get in front of a computer screen."

At the end of her work shift, Millie went home, took off her sandals, and opened her take-out salad. She carried it and a small bottle of sweet tea to the dining room table.

She ate her salad and looked at the clock, wondering if it was too late to go out again.

With the money that she'd earned from working at the Key Lime Garden Inn and the check that Maggie gave her upon her return, Millie had more than enough money to pay her rent.

She had one more thing to do before she turned in for the night, so as soon as she finished eating dinner, she set out once again.

DeWitt Pawn & Jewelry was still open when she pulled up in front of their store. She went inside and the little bell jingled.

The owner smiled when he saw her. "You're back."

Millie nodded. "I am. By any chance would my ring still be here?"

He turned and walked to his desk. Opening the top drawer, he took out a tiny clear plastic bag and handed it to her.

"You know, I've been in this business for over thirty years. I've met a lot of people and seen a lot of desperate behaviors. After a while, a person gets to recognize those who make a living pawning items, and those for whom life has dealt them a rough deal. I don't know what circumstance brought you here that day, but I know people. The minute you told me it was your mother's ring, I decided not to sell it. I knew you'd be back, and I'm glad."

Millie didn't understand why good fortune was suddenly following her, but she promised herself that she'd never take it for granted.

She opened her purse and took out one thousand dollars and handed it to the man. He placed her mother's ring in her hand, and said, "I hope I never see you again."

She looked up at him and smiled. "Thank you."

It wasn't enough just to sit in front of the computer monitor for an hour or so. Chelsea and her friends insisted they celebrate their lunch-bunch gathering complete with food and drink.

Chelsea stopped into Jerry's market to pick up finger food and a key lime pie, and Maggie brought two bottles of wine to the meeting.

Maggie didn't admonish herself for not creating some delectable concoction since she hadn't been given much notice about the meeting. She let Chelsea get the food, and she'd be responsible for the wine. Besides, only two of them would be in the room since it was virtual.

Looking over the kitchen table, Maggie asked, "How much food did you buy?"

"You've heard people say never go to the market when you're hungry? Well, I didn't listen. I've already been eating for the last two hours."

Maggie laughed. "In your defense, it's hard to resist stuff at Jerry's market. I love their summer pineapple slaw. Are the birds back?"

Jerry's had several parrots who greeted shoppers as they walked up the pathway to the market. They had been removed and taken to a safe place when the hurricane struck Sanibel and Captiva.

"They are. Gold Wing was ringing his bell and Jerry, Jr. squawked a bit and then said hello when I came by."

Chelsea set up the monitor at the end of the dining room table and Maggie poured white wine into their wine glasses.

Diana was the first to join them, followed by Kelly and Rachel.

"Hello, ladies," Chelsea said. "Maggie and I are here."

Maggie waved. "Nice to see everyone. How many months has it been?" she asked.

"I think six," Diana answered.

"I hate that life gets in the way," Kelly added.

"Rachel, how's life on Cape Cod?" Maggie asked.

"I love it here. Everly is thriving and, I think, so am I. It feels good to be back where I grew up, and the vineyard is a success too," Rachel answered. "How about you and Maggie? How's Captiva Island after the hurricane?"

Chelsea looked at Maggie. "Never a dull moment around here. The island has come back better than before. We're lucky there wasn't extensive damage this time."

"Who knows what the damage will be soon. My mother is coming to live here," Maggie said through laughter.

"Oh my goodness, Maggie, is that a good thing?" Kelly asked.

"Actually, I think it will be, but time will tell. I would rather have her close by than up in Massachusetts where I can't check on her to be honest."

Jane's face appeared and everyone clapped. "The woman of the hour finally shows up," Chelsea teased.

"Hey, just because I'm engaged doesn't mean I'm not still as busy with work as ever. How is everyone?"

"We were just catching up. So far, if there is any drama or

gossip we need to discuss, we've waited for you before bringing it up," Maggie added.

"Don't have any gossip, but I see everyone has a glass of wine. That's perfect because we need to celebrate and plan. Maggie, I hope Chelsea has explained the reason for today's meeting?"

Maggie smiled and nodded. "She did say something about a bachelorette party down here on Captiva. We were laughing about my bachelorette party and how Rachel went into labor with Everly while we were in the middle of the ocean."

Rolling her eyes, Rachel said, "Don't remind me. I couldn't believe it when my water broke on the top deck."

"Well, let's figure out when we can make this happen, and then we'll get to catching up on everyone's family news," Jane said.

"Did you want just us for the party or do you have any other women that you want to join us?"

"Only my sister Natalie, she'll be my Matron of Honor. So, we're talking seven women. I'm thinking of a long weekend down your way the weekend of June 10th."

Maggie scratched her head. "I'll have had a wedding at the inn the weekend before, but I think that will work. We'll just finish with one celebration and start another."

Chelsea looked at Maggie. "What's happening on June 3rd?"

"Ciara and Crawford picked that day for their wedding and they want to have it at the inn."

"Oh, this will be fun. So much to look forward to," Chelsea said.

Maggie shrugged. "Maybe more than you know. Lauren is due June 12th."

"Oh, no you don't. We can't have another baby interrupting our fun," Jane teased.

"I wouldn't worry about it. First of all, Lauren is in Massachusetts and the rest of us will be down here. The most that will happen is that I get a phone call letting me know she's in labor or the baby has arrived."

"Whew," Diana said. "That would have been hilarious if she was with us and went into labor."

"Okay, I guess that's settled. I hate to put this on everyone but as far as the planning goes, I want you all to figure that out. Surprise me. I might be forty-nine, but this is my first time getting married. I'm going for all the traditional stuff," Jane said.

"How about we just use all the leftover wedding stuff from Ciara's wedding?" Maggie teased.

"Very funny," Jane answered.

"So, let's get to the details. How did the dentist... what's his name...propose?" Kelly asked.

"His name is Brian Dever. He's very romantic. Since my dad is gone, he went to my brother Kevin and asked for my hand. Isn't that the cutest? Then, when we went skiing out in Utah, he asked me on the ski lift. He knows how much I love skiing, so he thought it would be a great memory-maker. He did it again at the ski lodge in front of a bunch of people around the fire."

"That's interesting," Maggie said. "I wonder why he proposed twice?"

"Oh, that made perfect sense. We had on these clunky ski gloves and he was terrified that he'd drop the ring if he gave it to me on the lift."

The women all nodded. "Smart guy. I would have killed him if my engagement ring fell into a snow bank," Chelsea said.

"I notice you've been keeping your hand out of view. Let's see the ring," Rachel said.

Jane held her hand in front of the camera for everyone to see.

"Holy cow. That thing is bigger than your knuckle," Chelsea said.

Maggie looked at Chelsea with a disapproving face. "That's not very nice."

"I'm sorry, but have you ever seen a diamond…is that diamond yellow?"

Everyone laughed at Chelsea's usual bluntness. "It is," Jane said. "It's eight-and-a-half carats and is a yellow diamond."

"Okay, I take back any bad thing I've ever said about dentists," Chelsea joked.

"Come on, ladies. Raise your glass to Jane and Brian. We never thought this day would come but we're so glad that it has. We love you. Congratulations!" Maggie declared.

Everyone raised their glass and cheered. It was the best lunch-bunch get-together in a long time. Maggie was pleased that she'd made the time to see her friends once again. These women had been her best friends when she lived in Massachusetts, and she missed hearing from them.

For the next forty-five minutes, they chatted about everything under the sun. Diana was conflicted about closing her bakery. Rachel talked about her baby and her sisters who helped her run the vineyard. Her author sister, Lucy, would be making a movie from one of her books. Kelly talked about her children and was still wearing her blue topaz dangling earrings.

Maggie's life was getting back to normal after such a tumultuous month, and soon, she would have a furry friend to talk to when she'd take her early morning walks. She couldn't wait.

aggie was outside in the garden with Paolo when she heard the car come up the driveway. Kathleen Hannagan, along with a tall man, got out of the car.

"Hello, Kathleen. It's good to see you again," Maggie said as Paolo took off his gloves and joined them in the driveway. "This is my husband, Paolo."

Paolo and Maggie shook Kathleen and the man's hand.

"This is my husband, Adam," Kathleen said.

"Welcome to the Key Lime Garden Inn and our home. I assume you are looking for Millie?" Maggie asked.

"Yes, we first stopped by her place but when she wasn't there, we thought we'd find her working here today."

"Why don't I go get her…" Maggie said and then stopped when she saw Millie on the back porch holding a stack of towels.

"There she is. Millie, come down here," Maggie yelled.

Millie put the towels on a chair and walked down the steps to the driveway.

"Hello, Millie," Kathleen said. "This is my husband, Adam. He wanted to meet you."

Millie smiled and nodded. "Nice to meet you, Adam."

Kathleen pulled out a paper from her purse and handed it to Millie.

"The results came in this morning. I've been going to Ancestry's website every day and nothing was there. I kept hitting refresh, and finally this morning, this showed up. I didn't know if you'd have time to look online while you were working, so we decided to drive out here to give you the news."

Millie looked at the printout and saw that along with several other people who were first, second and third cousins, Kathleen's name was at the very top showing that she indeed was Millie's sister.

Millie looked at the couple standing before her and tried not to cry. It was too late as tears were already falling on her face. Kathleen was crying too. The sisters threw their arms around each other and hugged. Adam put his hand on Millie's back. "Welcome to our family, Millie."

Maggie and Paolo congratulated everyone on the good news.

"We are thrilled for all of you," Maggie said.

"Even though I was an only child, we have tons of cousins and family who Millie hasn't met yet," Kathleen said.

"Yes, so we're going to put together a big barbeque and invite everyone in the family. They have to meet Millie and she, them," Adam added.

Smiling, Maggie said, "I think that's wonderful. Millie, why don't you get out of here and go spend the day with your family. I can finish putting things away."

"Are you sure?" Millie asked.

"Of course. Get out of here. We'll see you tomorrow."

Millie looked at Kathleen. "I've got my car, though."

"You can leave it here and come back for it later. Go on, get going,"

Millie ran inside, and Maggie and Paolo said their goodbyes to the Hannagans.

Millie ran down the stairs, hugged Maggie and Paolo, and

followed Kathleen and Adam to their car. As they sped away, Millie turned to look out the back window and waved.

Paolo went back to the garden, and Maggie went into the kitchen and made a pot of tea.

Standing at the back door, Chelsea said, "Who are you planning to lecture now?"

"Lecture? What are you talking about?" Maggie asked.

"You don't usually make a pot of tea unless you're getting ready to sit someone down and force them to listen to unsolicited advice."

"I know I've got a reputation, but once in a while I like to make tea for myself. But, now that you mention it, now that you're here, do you need any of my brilliant words of wisdom?"

"No, thanks. I got a boat-load from your mother. Unlike you, her words kind of stick with a person," Chelsea said.

"I have no idea what that means, and I don't care to. So, what's going on with you?" Maggie asked.

Just then, Paolo came up on the porch carrying a basket of newly picked kale and tomatoes. "Good morning, Chelsea."

"Hey, Paolo. Looks like you've got something good for Riley to make for dinner tonight."

"Could be. We never know exactly what she and Iris plan. I just pick what needs picking and they run with it," he said.

"So, since you're both here, I've decided something and I thought I'd let you know," Chelsea said.

"Oh?" Maggie responded.

"I've decided to go to Key West to see my sisters. It will probably only be for a few days, maybe a long weekend. I figure we shouldn't let too much time go before we try to fix things between us."

Maggie put her hand on Chelsea's. "I think that's a wonderful idea, Chelsea."

"Good for you," Paolo added. "These things can fester and get worse if you don't make the effort. I wish you great success."

Chelsea smiled. "Thanks, Paolo. I've decided something else. I'm going to give my sisters money to get started. I can't give them as much as Sebastian did, but it will be enough to make a difference. I might as well get used to eating humble pie."

She looked at Maggie who had a huge smile on her face. "What do you think about coming with me? I could use the support."

Maggie looked at Paolo. "What do you think?"

"Don't look at me," he said. "You don't need my permission."

Maggie laughed. "There is no way in the world I want to miss watching you eat humble pie. I would pay money to see that. When do we leave?"

"How does the day after tomorrow sound?" Chelsea answered.

"Sounds perfect. Let's go inside and have some of that tea. I've got lots of advice for you before we go. You don't just want to show up without a plan," Maggie explained as she went inside.

Chelsea looked at Paolo. "Your wife is really something."

Paolo smiled. "Don't I know it."

After Chelsea left, Maggie walked into the laundry room and saw what Millie had left behind. Several sheets, pillow cases, and towels were in piles on the floor. She filled the washing machine with the first load and then moved the vacuum cleaner that was in the middle of the hall into the library.

Maggie had asked Millie to bring down additional blankets that were stored in the attic, but when she looked at them sitting on top of the dryer, she realized that Millie had selected the ones meant for Christmas decorations. It was an easy mistake to make. *My bad. I should have explained better.*

She pulled the attic stairs down and gathered up two blankets at a time, throwing them overhead. When all the blankets had been tossed above, she climbed up to put them back in the proper plastic bin.

She folded each one, put them back where they belonged and went looking for the bin that was labeled "extra blankets." She noticed that the box she had set aside with Rose and Robert Lane's items had been moved, and the large, plastic bag with their hair brushes inside sat on top. Maggie sat on the floor in front of it, picked up the bag, and saw a note underneath. In a black marker, the note read:

Dear Maggie,

I will never be able to thank you for everything you did for me. You were right. Families come in all shapes and sizes. I'm so glad that I'm part of yours.

Millie

Maggie smiled as she placed the bag back inside the box. She pushed it back into the corner, folded Millie's note, and put it in her pocket. She then walked to the window and looked outside at her garden, and thought, *Yes, they do, Millie. They certainly do.*

THE END

ALSO BY ANNIE CABOT

THE CAPTIVA ISLAND SERIES

Book One: KEY LIME GARDEN INN

Book Two: A CAPTIVA WEDDING

Book Three: CAPTIVA MEMORIES

Book Four: CAPTIVA CHRISTMAS

Book Five: CAPTIVA NIGHTS

Book Six: CAPTIVA HEARTS

Book Seven: CAPTIVA EVER AFTER

For a **FREE** copy of the Prequel to the Captiva Island Series, **Captiva Sunset** - Join my newsletter HERE.

THE PERIWINKLE SHORES SERIES

Book One: CHRISTMAS ON THE CAPE

Book Two: THE SEA GLASS GIRLS

ACKNOWLEDGMENTS

With each book I continue to be grateful to the people who support my work. I couldn't do what I do without them. Thank you all so much.

Cover Design: Marianne Nowicki
Premade Ebook Cover Shop
https://www.premadeebookcovershop.com/

Editor: Lisa Lee of Lisa Lee Proofreading and Editing
https://www.facebook.com/EditorLisaLee/

Beta Readers:
John Battaglino
Nancy Burgess
Michele Connolly
Anne Marie Page Cooke

ABOUT THE AUTHOR

Annie Cabot is the author of contemporary women's fiction and family sagas. Annie writes about friendships and family relationships, that bring inspiration and hope to others.

Annie Cabot is the pen name for the writer Patricia Pauletti (Patti) who was a co-author of several paranormal mystery books under the pen name Juliette Harper.

A lover of all things happily ever after, it was only a matter of time before she began to write what was in her heart, and so, the pen name Annie Cabot was born.

When she's not writing, Annie and her husband like to travel. Winters always involve time away on Captiva Island, Florida where she continues to get inspiration for her novels.

Annie lives in Massachusetts with her husband and an adorable new puppy named Willa.

For more information visit anniecabot.com